HIS STUBBORN BEAR

BEARS OF ASHEVILLE BOOK 1

SKYE R. RICHMOND

*For My Awesome Readers If You Run Into A Bear It's
Definitely Not A Hot Guy, Don't Be Like Kian!*

RUN!!

Cover Art: Cosmic Letterz

Edited by M.A. Hinkle

Proofreading By: Karen Meeus

Sign up for Skye's newsletter for exclusive content and to learn more about her latest books: https://www. rhelandrichmond.com/newsletter

1

KIAN

ALL THE BOOKS TOLD YOU NOT TO MAKE HUGE DECISIONS after a major loss. But I needed to get out of there. Between losing my papa and ending things with Danny, I just needed a fresh start.

In Montana, though! Really, Kian! Really?

I didn't know crap about ranching. Plus, I was a little scared of anything bigger than a teacup poodle. It wasn't like I couldn't rebuild and rebrand the websites and branding at home. *Not that you have one anymore.* Yeah, maybe selling the family house after Papa died hadn't been my smartest idea. But God, without him, it just hadn't felt like home anymore. It hadn't felt like the home I'd grown up in with both my parents gone.

And I couldn't exactly ask Danny to vacate the condo we shared, especially being the one that had ended things. I could still see the confusion in his eyes. We'd grown comfortable and complacent in our relationship, but as I was walking away from the only place I'd known and into the unknown, I couldn't help but wonder—was that such a bad thing? Then again, did I want forever with someone that was more like a permanent roommate? We rarely even had sex anymore. I couldn't even remember our last date... There had never been a time I thought there would be a gaping hole in his heart if I was gone. And maybe that was asking for too much...but I was asking.

Now wasn't the time to be asking those questions. The time would have been a month ago. Heck, even two weeks ago.

I shook off that thought and looked at the GPS. "Thirty minutes away." I wasn't far from the town of Asheville, Montana. The last few miles had been nothing but green, rolling hills and land as far as the eye could see, and wow, was the countryside beautiful. Open fields and clear skies. I bet that even the air smelled fresh, nothing like the city.

You're not in Philly anymore, Kian.

I didn't believe in fate, but when my best friend from college, Rhys, called after Papa passed away to offer his condolences, we'd talked for hours. Just like we always did. Time never seemed to pass with him. Even though it had been almost a year since we spoke on the phone and several years seeing each other in person.

Which was your fault. Rhys had tried calling me several times, but I hadn't been in the mood to talk.

He'd moved back to Montana after school, and we'd kept in touch via email, phone calls, and FaceTime. But even those had stopped almost completely on my end after Papa became sick.

That gut-wrenching feeling hit me again. Even though I knew it was coming, it didn't stop it from hurting any less. No matter how many times I'd told myself he was with Dad now, it still felt like I was being sucked into oblivion with pain.

My hands tightened around the wheel. Yeah, I definitely needed a fresh start. Besides, I had Daddy and Papa with me. Their ashes were mixed, so now they were together in death as they had been in life.

You're still all alone in the world.

Ignoring that nagging voice had become a daily exercise. Especially when it called me silly for leaving Danny and the comfort of stability to start somewhere new. Truthfully, I wanted what my parents had. It was like they'd breathed in sync. Dad had treated Papa like he was the center of the universe and everything revolved around him. I wanted that. That kind of love and devotion... It wasn't too much to ask, was it?

That thought wasn't getting me anywhere. I was focusing on the future and the move. Even though moving without a place to live wasn't the best idea.

Yeah, 'cause when you're less than twenty minutes away is a good time to realize that.

It wasn't technically starting from scratch. I knew Rhys. From the moment we'd met on the first day of orientation, he had taken me under his wing and taken care of me. Sometimes, I forgot I was older than him by a couple of months.

He was my one true friend. *More like your only friend.* While I'd never been good at the whole "making friends" thing, Rhys hadn't really given me a choice; he'd declared us 'besties.' His actual words had been, "We're going to be best friends. I just know it."

I had thought he was crazy, or worse, he'd see me and decide I wasn't worth it. I'd been terrified college would be as sucky as high school, so I went with it, all the while waiting for the other shoe to drop. However, it never did. Instead, he'd made four years of college that could have been utterly unbearable…wonderful.

He'd come over to my house a lot since I used to live in-state. However, this was going to be my first time at his house, despite being invited several times in the past. *And you said no. But here you are, moving without ever even having been to Montana.*

Well, I was here now. That was when I saw the sign that read 'Asheville' and underneath it 'Population: 1,928.' Fuck, I'd never been to a town that small. Rhys hadn't been exaggerating when he said everyone knew each other.

Maybe this was a bad idea. I'd be the new guy, sticking out like a sore thumb. Shit… *Well, you're here now, and it's not like you have anything to return to.*

As a freelance graphic and web designer, most of my work was virtual. So technically, I could live anywhere with Internet access. Asheville just had someone that felt like family. *Rhys is family. Breathe.* I repeated those words to myself over and over.

As I got into what I guessed was downtown, I was surprised to find that it wasn't anything like I expected. For such a small town, everything looked stunning. Main Street actually looked like something out of a postcard. A very Dutch postcard.

They even had a windmill. How had I never heard of this town? It was like stepping into Europe. Hold on, was that a chocolatier? And a gelato shop? Maybe I should have taken the time to look up my new home because it looked like I wasn't ending up in the Middle of Nowheresville, Montana.

I followed the GPS until I arrived at the large arch that read 'Crazy Bear Mountain Ranch.' I shook my head at the name and made a mental note to ask Rhys what on earth had inspired it. Especially since it was also the name of the company.

Though I guessed it was working for them since you couldn't walk into a store without finding their pastries, milk, beef, sausages, meatballs, and several other beef and dairy products with their name on them.

I still couldn't believe I would get to work on their whole rebrand.

It was huge for me. A game changer, really.

As I drove up the road to the ranch, I wondered if I should call Rhys and go over to his house first. This seemed like the business's location. And since he'd hired me, maybe meeting him and having him take me to the boss was the way to go.

Although I'd spoken to him before I set off this morning after my last stop at a motel six hours away, and then he had told me to meet here.

As the sprawling ranch house appeared, I shrugged. I was already here. And wow, it was massive. Several other houses also sat on the property.

There were also several trucks, SUVs, and one Mini Cooper parked on both sides of the house. So I parked next to the Mini and immediately breathed a sigh of relief for making it here in one piece.

It felt like something so small, but I was proud of myself for making the drive down myself. Rhys had volunteered to fly up and have us drive down together, but I'd told him I was fine.

I wanted to do it myself. Prove I could do it. It wasn't like I had anyone else in the world to depend on. It was just me, myself, and I. But I could do this.

Before I could even get my phone out, my door was yanked open, and a grinning Rhys greeted me. He looked just the way I remembered him with his sparkling brown eyes and his thick, wavy brown hair. He wore it slightly longer on top now. He'd even grown a beard, although he kept it neatly trimmed and tapered. Slightly more than a stubble. It suited him.

"Kian." The excitement in his voice and his huge

smile washed over me, and I knew I had made the right choice.

I got out of the car, and immediately, Rhys slung his arms around me. "Oh my days, Kee. I'm so glad you're here. I can't believe we're going to be living together like the old days. How exciting is that? I moved in by myself a while ago, but it's weird living alone." I let Rhys's continued to babble excitedly and I simply grinned at my friend.

I'd had flashes of doubt as I'd driven here, but seeing Rhys again, I felt better.

The hairs on the back of my neck suddenly stood, and goose bumps sprang up all over me. I could feel eyes on me. I looked over to the entrance and found a large man with a disapproving look on his face. When our gazes met, they held for a second, and his eyes widened. He pressed down on his chest like it hurt. It looked like he took a step towards me, but then he shook his head before spinning around and heading back into the house.

It looks like one of them doesn't want you here.

It seemed I shouldn't expect a warm reception from everyone, but Rhys was excited. That was enough. I still couldn't help wondering which of his brothers that was. I'd met Graham, but there was also Hunter and... Gabe, and one more. His name escaped me now.

I shook off the encounter and wrapped my arms around Rhys and sighed. "Me too. Me too."

2

GABE

I PUSHED MY HANDS THROUGH MY HAIR FOR WHAT FELT like the fiftieth time in the last twenty minutes. Rhys refused to see reason.

"Okay, I see why we need to hire him." I shook my head. "Actually, I don't, but one thing at a time. Why couldn't you find a place for him in town?"

Rhys raised a brow. "He's my best friend, so why shouldn't he stay with me? I have a whole house. Not like there's anyone else here to share it with."

"Rhys," I sighed. My youngest brother was and had always been very stubborn. When he set his mind to something, he was immovable. *Like you, you mean.* I shook the thought away. Definitely not touching that one.

I supposed being the first child did that to me, but that meant I couldn't blame Rhys as the youngest and only omega. I knew he had to find a way to make his voice heard, and boy, had he! But this time, I was putting my foot down.

"You know I'm right," I insisted, refusing to be swayed. "A human on the ranch." The thought of it had the hairs on my neck standing.

"So? We have humans in town." Rhys folded his arms with that unyielding look that said he would not budge.

"Oh, stop it," I said. "You know that's different since they're mated." I begged Urs for patience so I didn't say *because I said so and that's final.* "It's different, and you know it," I repeated with insistence.

"Well, maybe Kian will find his mate too." Rhys shrugged. "He has no one. Can you imagine Papa and Dad gone? And then what if you didn't have any of us?"

I closed my eyes, trying to dispel the thought. My family was everything. Not having them... I refused to even think about it.

"See." Rhys sounded triumphant. "You know I'm right."

I leaned back and shook my head. "Rhys, I hear you, and I feel bad for him, but having a human on the ranch is bad for everyone. What if he sees one of us?"

Rhys shrugged as if the answer was easy. "Then we tell him." My brother uncrossed and crossed his legs again. "I always wanted to, but I couldn't exactly shift in the dorm. I figured when he came up here, I would."

I shook my head. "Okay, let's table that for a moment." I rubbed my brow. "I can see you're not in the mood to listen. But why do we even need to change anything? The brand is doing great; the last quarter was possibly our best."

My brother sighed dramatically, throwing his hands in the air. "Seriously! Have you been to our website? It's a miracle we even have any clients. It looks like something created on Blogspot in 2000." He huffed. "And that's me being kind... Just, no. We can do better. Our social media presence is almost nonexistent."

"That is the last thing we need. We keep a low profile, remember?" I pointed out, brow raised. "Besides, we provide great, high-quality products at excellent prices. Since when isn't that enough?"

"Uhh, first of all, don't act like I said we should put up a video of us shifting on the internet. Okay?" He rolled his eyes, "And just for the record, branding became, like, a major thing since influencing became the norm. You gotta keep up, bro." Rhys sighed and, without uttering the words, managed to call me 'silly old big brother.' "Sure, we're in the big chains, but I have plans for gourmet orders. Or even a subscription service and so much more," Rhys went on. "For all that to happen, we need to get with the times."

I didn't hate any of those ideas. But it took me back to my initial argument.

"I hear you on all of this, and I agree. We *could* do with a little update," I conceded.

"A little?" Rhys snorted.

Ignoring him, I went on, "But why does he have to

even be in town? Isn't all this graphic stuff done online now? Why can't we do that?"

"I told you why, Gabe." Rhys huffed. "Honestly, do you even listen?"

I issued a warning growl. As much as Rhys was making light of things, it was my job to keep my people safe. I wasn't mayor like my brother Austin or even Sheriff like Hunter, but I was still the alpha since Dad stepped down. Therefore, it was my job to keep my town, my home, my people, *my family* safe, and that meant shielding us from the prying eyes of humans.

Why didn't Rhys get this?

"Can we at least not do anything too fast?" I suggested.

Suddenly, Rhys seemed to find a spot in his pants very interesting.

"Rhyssss!" I knew what that look meant, especially since my brother wouldn't meet my eyes. I sighed and rubbed my brow.

"How long?" I asked.

"Well," Rhys said. "Hmm, in about an hour." He pulled his phone out. "Kian let me into his Find My Phone account so I could track his journey. It's his first time driving on his own, you know. Did I mention he was my roommate in college? Kian is the sweetest. Trust me, he couldn't hurt a fly. Actually scratch that, thirty minutes."

My brain stalled on the thirty minutes. My brother had only told me about this three days ago, and even then, it had been couched as a suggestion. I'd told him I would think about it, but clearly, it was a done deal.

"Let me guess, you already hired him?"

"Well…" His voice trailed off.

"Dammit, Rhys! You know better. I know you know better," I snapped.

"I do." My brother folded his arms. "Which is why I know this is the right thing. Kian is family, and if he were a member of the den, then we would welcome him."

"But he's not. He's human," I reminded him. "It would be different if he was a shifter, half-shifter, or even had a shifter somewhere in his family tree."

"But—" he tried.

"No, Rhys. This is dangerous. The last thing we need is for him to accidentally see something and run away screaming or worse. What if this whole social media thing catches something it's not supposed to?"

My brother snorted, and I narrowed my eyes at him.

"You know that's not how it works, right?" he said. "It doesn't magically appear on the 'Gram. You have to post it."

I blew out a breath. "At least keep him in town. We know no one is going to shift in the middle of town."

Rhys shook his head. "I can't." He leaned forward, his eyes serious. "Kian doesn't do well in new places. Or with new people. He's shy. I've always watched out for him."

Fuck.

"How would it look if I suddenly told him, 'Actually, you can't stay at my house. You have to stay in a bed-and-breakfast.' I know Kee, and he'll think he's done something wrong. Besides, he should be around someone that cares about him after everything he's been through."

I couldn't fault Rhys's argument, but it still didn't mean I was wrong.

"Do Papa and Dad know?" I asked.

"Yup, they think it's fine. They met Kian a couple of times when they came down to visit," Rhys said. "You would have too if you had ever come."

"You know why I couldn't," I defended.

He waved me off. "Yeah. Yeah, I wasn't bitching at you. I'm just saying if you'd met him, you'd know you had nothing to worry about. That's all."

"Fine." I knew when I was beaten. "But make sure everyone knows to shift further out, not close to the house, okay?"

Rhys's grin was triumphant. "You're the best, Gabe."

I rolled my eyes. The little shit knew he would get his way. He'd been doing it since he was a little boy and he realized batting those lashes at me would get him what he wanted.

My phone pinged, and I picked it up from the desk to see it was a message from Rhys in our family chat. I raised a brow at him as I opened it.

Rhys: Guest on Ranch. Don't shift near the house.

Really? Shaking my head, I started typing.

Gabe: Human guest on Ranch. He'll be working here a while. Be aware and try to shift as far away from where you can be seen.

Rhys snorted. "I think they got my point."

I didn't even bother responding. I was over-cautious—I knew it—but we'd kept our secrets for a long time. It wouldn't be on my watch when they came out. Humans had proven over and over they couldn't be trusted with knowledge of our existence. We'd seen how they treated anything that was not like them.

Austin: Got it.

Graham: NP.

Hunter: Duly Noted.

Papa: You worry too much. What have I told you about everything going exactly as it should?

Dad: Told you it would be fine, son.

Rhys: Thanks, Dad. I know, right?

Of course, my parents encouraged him and left me to clean up the mess.

Graham: Kian is lovely. I'm sure everything will be fine.

Hunter: Is Gabe stewing? I should have bet he'd blow his top.

I growled, and Rhys chuckled even as I saw him typing a message.

Rhys: He can't say no to me. I'm his favorite.

I snorted. He wasn't wrong—he was everyone's favorite; it had to do with the whole *only omega* and *last child* thing.

Gabe: I'm signing out.

Rhys: You do know this is not MSN Messenger. Right?

Austin: Ha.

Graham: Does he even know what that is?

Hunter: LMAO!!!

I put the phone down and glared at Rhys but only got a smile for my trouble.

"How about you go to your office and leave me in peace?" I looked pointedly at the door.

Rhys slouched further into his seat. "Nope, my day is clear... Oh my gosh, he's here." Rhys jumped up. "Kee just pulled up."

I sighed and said a prayer to whoever was listening that this didn't end in disaster.

"Come on, he probably has a ton of stuff. Let's go help him." My brother was out of the office before I could blink.

I huffed and considered calling for someone else to help with the bags. We'd converted the original ranch house to the offices and meeting places for den members, amongst other things. So there was always someone around. But I figured I might as well go see what Rhys had gotten us into.

I watched at the door as Rhys enveloped a smaller man into his arms. My brother was five nine, which was short in comparison to the rest of us, but this man was much shorter.

When Rhys leaned him away from his body and he smiled, my belly did a weird flip. I took a step forward, trying to get a better look at his profile. The next thing I knew, he turned and looked my way, and our eyes met and held. My heart began to race.

When the breeze picked up and the most tantalizing

scent hit my nostrils, my bear roared. It couldn't be... Could it? It wasn't possible. It just wasn't.

Everything in my body screamed to go towards this man and wrap him up in my arms and never let go.

Mate! Mate! Mate!

Instead, I spun around and went back into the house.

Holy fuck. I was so screwed.

Even with that thought, a small smile spread across my face. I had a mate. And he was here.

He was here, a human omega, and Rhys's best friend.

Shit.

3

KIAN

I LOOKED AROUND RHYS'S HOME AND SMILED. IT WAS very welcoming. Not that it surprised me. Our dorm room had never felt like one, thanks to Rhys's efforts. Rhys had done his home in all earth tones and warm colors. From the two large sofas that looked like they'd be wonderful for an afternoon nap or curled with your feet under you while you read a book to the matching occasional chairs. Then, of course, there were blankets across the arms of each chair, along with chunky pillows, and not the ones you wanted to toss on the floor because they were annoying.

The largest couch faced a wall with a large television, but on both sides of it were shelves littered with books and what looked like a million photo frames of smiling people. That pang of sadness washed over me. I'd always wondered what it would be like to have siblings. I knew my parents had tried, but they always said they'd gotten it right on the first try. Almost as if Rhys could sense my mood, he reappeared from where he'd disappeared with my bags after telling me to make myself at home.

"You okay?" Rhys asked as he came into the living room. He furrowed his brows as he studied me.

I chuckled because this was the Rhys I knew. When we were in school, it was like he could always read my feelings. If I came back from class upset, he would know. And suddenly, he'd have something fun for us to do.

"I'm good," I reassured him. "You just have a beautiful family." I nodded at the pictures.

Rhys chuckled, looked over at the shelf, and grinned. "Loud too, but trust me. They're your family now too."

He pulled me in for a side hug, and I tried not to sniff, even as emotions overwhelmed me. I'd been almost certain I made the right call coming here; now, I was sure.

Rhys was the brother I'd always wanted.

However, the man from earlier flashed into my mind, and there was something about the intense way he had stared at me. From where I'd stood, he'd looked huge. Like, fill out the doorway, broad and tall.

I licked my lips, thinking about all those muscles, then shook it off. Nope, the last thing I needed to do was jump into a relationship right after everything that had happened.

I was definitely certain that was a no-no after losing your papa and ending an almost two-year relationship.

Not like he'll even want you, Kian. So don't even go there. That's not why you're here.

Rhys interrupted my thoughts. "So I can either show you around, or you can rest, and we'll have dinner later. Your choice."

I thought about it. "I'm not really tired, so how about a little tour?"

Rhys grinned and linked our arms together, and we headed down a hallway, then pushed the door that opened into a kitchen.

"The fridge and freezer are fully stocked," Rhys said. "Feel free to raid either and make whatever you want any time. Seriously, treat this as your place too."

We'd already had this argument, but I felt the need to say again, "You know I can pay rent or even contribute to the utilities."

Rhys shook his head and bumped my hip lightly. "Nope. But if you want, you can grab groceries if anything is running low. I will, too, although I forget easily. If you forget too, there's always food at my parents'. By the way, they can't wait to see you. Papa says you need a hug."

I smiled because this was something I'd missed about my bestie. Rhys babbled when he was excited.

"Have I mentioned how thrilled I am that you're here?" he asked.

"Once or twice," I teased with a chuckle. "But I'm so happy I'm here too."

"Good, now come on." Rhys opened a door on the other side of the kitchen, not the one I could see led to a fenced-in garden. Instead, we stepped into a garage. Rhys unlinked our arms.

"Where did I keep that key?" he muttered to himself.

"We could take my car. It's still out front," I reminded him even as I shook my head because this was another very Rhys thing to do. I looked left, then right, and of course, there was a key holder.

"By any chance, are these the keys you're looking for?" I asked, trying not to laugh as I slipped a set of keys off the hook.

He tapped his forehead. "Duh. Why do I never check there first?"

This was definitely a familiar conversation, so I simply laughed and tossed the keys over. As usual, Rhys caught them, even though I kinda sucked at the throw.

"All right, let's boogie." Rhys pulled a tarp off, and my mouth dropped open.

I looked at him, then back at the vehicle, then back at him, and found Rhys beaming with pride.

"Is that one of those mini kid cars for adults?" I asked. I couldn't keep the surprise from my voice as I was looking at perhaps a black Mini Jeep? I wasn't sure what it was.

"No, silly." Rhys walked over and patted it like a proud papa. "It's a UTV, kind of like an ATV but not."

"Uhhh?" I raised a brow because that wasn't really an explanation.

Rhys chuckled and got in, bidding, "Come on."

I walked over and saw that it did look like one of those things you saw people on safaris riding in. But this one only seated two. I opened the low doors and got in, surprised to see it had seatbelts and even a display console.

I looked up to find Rhys's eyes on me. "Buckle up," he said.

I shook my head at the excited gleam in his eyes. "Did you just get this?"

He nodded, smiling. "Yup, came in two days ago, been dying to take it out." Rhys turned on the engine and caressed the wheel like a lover. "She's a beauty, right? 2021 Yamaha Wolverine RMAX 1000." He said it like I would know what that meant. "I was going to get the Honda Pioneer since it's got space for kids and all, but since I'm fresh out of those, this will have to do. By the way, I should tell you—the dating pool around here is nonexistent. I shoulda given you that heads-up before you packed up, huh?"

There was something in my friend's voice, but when I looked over at him, he fiddled with something and refused to look my way. Before I could ask Rhys if he wanted to talk, the garage door opened. "All right, let's get this show on the road." And we were off.

"It's not as loud as I thought it would be," I said as we pulled out of the garage.

Rhys nodded and smiled. "I know, right? It gets louder on other settings, but since we're just driving around the living area, there's no need to show off those yet."

"Do I need one of these?" I asked. "Because my Kia is cute and all, but I don't think it was made for all-terrain."

"Nah, you don't need one. Besides, if you ever do, we have a couple you can borrow. You can drive up in your car to the main house, where you arrived," he added for clarification. "I've just been dying to use this. Plus, it's great when you want to drive out further to the unpaved parts of the land...like the meadow, river, and such. Oooh, we'll totally have to go swimming."

I laughed. "Of course you have," I said. "Wait, hold on. How many acres do you guys own?"

"Hmm, well, this part is about six hundred acres. Originally, the property was two thousand, but my great-grandpa developed houses on the eastern part of the land. It's got its own entrance, and it's kind of cut off from our parts now, but only kind of. We like to let den—I mean, the town needed the houses, so we donated part of our land. That was also about the time when we stopped raising cattle."

"I was going to ask if you did," I said.

"Nope, not anymore. Pop-pop focused on the

factory. His brother, my uncles and cousins who live a few towns over, they still do, though."

We finally got moving, far enough for Rhys to point out the important landmarks of the tour. "All right, so enough town history. Let's introduce you to your neighbors," Rhys said. "Next to us on the left is Graham, my immediate older brother."

"I remember Graham," I said. He'd visited Rhys more than once while we were at college.

"Yeah, so he's on the left of me, and on the right is Hunter. You've not met him yet. He's the sheriff in town. As you can see, they stuck me right in the middle to keep an eye on me."

I snorted at how petulant he sounded but took in the houses he pointed out. They were beautiful, and I couldn't help wondering what it would be like to live right next door to your siblings. Family in general, to be honest. I'd been an only child of only children, so it was just me now.

Looking around at all this, I found I was a little jealous of how close Rhys and his family were.

I shook off that feeling; jealousy was a wasted emotion, my papa would say. Besides, it's not like it would do me any good.

Instead, I focused on my surroundings. Unlike the main building I'd pulled up at, these homes weren't made of logs and brick. It'd looked more like I'd wound up in one of those fancy gated estates. Studying the house, it seemed they were all versions of modern farmhouses, ranch-style and craftsman homes mish-mashed together. The brothers seemed to have taken what they liked from each one. But even though they all looked similar, they actually weren't. It was subtle, but each brother seemed to personalize their home with something unique. I really liked the white with grey trim Rhys had gone for. It was peaceful, modern but homey. Then there was one that was white with a beautiful light wood trim. But my favorite had to the one with the raised front porch framed with white columns and a stone stoop.

The houses were close enough together that a short walk to borrow a cup of sugar would be simple, but they weren't so close you could hear everything happening next door.

"The ones opposite ours act as guest houses for when family comes to visit, you know. We also have a lodge further out for huge gatherings, not that we've had one in a while." Rhys continued his narration as we drove forward. "This is Austin's, my second-oldest brother and the mayor."

I heard the pride in Rhys's voice. In fact, I heard it each time he mentioned one of his brothers.

"And opposite him is Gabe, my grouchy oldest brother. Of course, Papa and Dad are first on the street. Pops and Grandma have a cottage by the river, but at the moment, they're visiting family in Europe, or maybe they're on a cruise in Alaska. I can't keep up with them."

"Wow, it's amazing how you basically have three generations living together here," I said. "Must be nice having family around all the time."

"Yeah, it is, even when they're overbearing. I couldn't imagine not having them around."

Rhys's head whipped towards me, and he braked hard. Thankfully, the seatbelts held. Not that we were going fast enough to cause any damage. "Oh, my gosh. I'm so sorry, Kee. I didn't mean—"

"I know you didn't." I managed a smile. "I'm fine, honestly."

"I'm sorry," Rhys said again. He looked like a kicked puppy.

I smiled and pointed forward. "Drive."

Rhys nudged me one last time, and I shook my head, smiling.

He got moving, and in a low voice, he said, "You know you can talk about them anytime, right?"

My heart caught, but I nodded. "I know, but not now, okay?"

Rhys didn't reply. Instead, we left the family estate, and he pointed out bunkhouses, stables, and a number of animals, including cows, despite them not raising cows anymore. I would stay away from those. I'd read somewhere not to get cornered by a cow. Apparently, they could squish you... Although, maybe that was a dream... Either way, me and animals didn't mix. Even dogs scared me.

Even with the undesirable wildlife, I had to admit

that the land was stunning, and I was pretty sure I'd never seen this much green up close—ever. Maybe once on a school trip to Central Park. Even then, the air certainly hadn't been as fresh as it was here.

I knew with certainty that my parents would be proud of me for this decision. Sure, it'd been spur of the moment. But it was the right thing for me.

Some of the stress I'd been carrying since Papa took his final breath seeped away. The memory of holding his hand by his bedside gradually began to plague me less.

I was definitely glad to be out of Philly. By the time we pulled up in front of Rhys's parents' home, I said, "I totally get why we couldn't walk."

He laughed, turning the engine off and twisting to face me. "Did you think I was being a drama bear?"

"If the shoe fits," I teased.

Rhys rolled his eyes and hopped out again without opening the doors. Oh, to have long legs.

I opened the door and got out to meet Rhys on the other side of the vehicle. "I can't believe we drove ten miles and never left the property. That's crazy."

Rhys linked our arms again, and it warmed my heart. I'd forgotten how tactile he was, and the truth was I'd missed it. My ex wasn't really a touchy person, but my papa and dad had been. I grew up with a lot of laughter, smiles, and embraces, dancing together in the middle of making dinner. Even after we lost Dad, the laughter and joy had stayed, a little dimmer but always present. Then, when Pops got sick, all that died. Maybe I was grasping at straws, but it felt like joy lived here.

The door flung open, and the next thing I knew, Mr. Hallbjọrn engulfed me in a hug.

"Kian." Jonathan, the tall, stunning omega, was Rhys's papa, and he pulled me into another big hug. I sighed and wrapped my arms around him. Then, without warning or a way to stop them, tears rolled down my cheeks. Maybe it was being in the arms of a papa again.

"Oh, sweet child, you're not alone," he crooned in my ears, simply holding me on the porch of his home. "You're not alone." The more he said this, the more the tears flowed.

I had felt alone for the last few months. I really had.

He pulled back to meet my eyes and simply smiled. I suddenly felt so exposed and ducked my head. He chuckled and took my hands. "Come on, there's nothing some hot soup and crusty bread can't fix."

I saw where Rhys got it from. When I walked into the house, Stefan, Rhys's alpha dad, pulled me into a tight hug of his own, patting my back twice without saying a word. The look in his eyes said everything.

"Come on. Dinner is ready, son," Stefan said.

I smiled at the gruff words, filled with warmth. Stefan was a bear of a man, over six-three for sure. However, on every occasion we'd met, he'd been nothing but kind. Plus, the way he treated Jon made it obvious he was a softie.

I followed behind Stefan with Jon holding on to me into a large kitchen that smelled absolutely delicious. My stomach rumbled.

"Right on time, it seems," Jon said. "Go on and wash up. I'll just get the food on the table."

"Thank you," I said to Rhys's papa and walked over to the sink.

"Hey!" Rhys exclaimed. When I looked back, I saw my friend rubbing his butt.

"Wash up." Jonathan had his hands on his hip, and I snorted when my friend snatched another slice of the oven-fresh crusty bread and ran behind Stefan just as Jonathan waved the wooden spatula threateningly.

With every moment that passed, I smiled a little more than I had in what felt like forever, and I said a thank you to whatever God had thought to bring Rhys into my life when he did.

Stefan snorted and pushed his son towards the sink. "Little rascal." I washed up quickly and turned around in time to see Stefan and Jonathan sharing a kiss. As they pressed their foreheads, whispering to each other, my heart flipped. Seeing them together reminded me of my parents, but it also reminded me that I might never have that.

I sighed, and Rhys came over and nudged me in the hip. "Don't mind them; they get all mushy all the time." I looked over at my friend and caught a glimpse of longing there, but it was gone quickly as he smiled at me.

"Papa made beef stew with dumplings, and it's my favorite. The bread, ugh, so good," Rhys said. "'Cause I'm his favorite son."

"Oh, is Gabe here?" Jonathan asked, his tone teasing.

Rhys gasped and put his hands over his heart in mock indignation. "That hurts, Papa. Hurts."

I laughed at their antics. This was what it had been like with my parents.

"Sit down, drama bear." Jonathan pointed to the dining table in the kitchen. It was big enough to seat eight, and it looked like there were enough plates in the middle of the table for exactly that many people. Maybe I would meet the rest of Rhys's brothers. Also, what was with this family and bears? Even their company referenced it: Crazy Bear Ranch. It stood out for sure, and I already had an idea for the branding but still, bears? Weird.

"Wow, this is enough to feed twenty," I said when the big bowl of soup was placed on the table.

"Or six hungry bears," Stefan snorted. Jonathan smacked him with the back of his hand, and they shared a look I couldn't decipher. I was even more confused when Rhys also laugh-snorted as he began scooping soup into his bowl.

"Don't mind him, Kian. Go on, dish up, eat, eat." He nodded at the bowl as he put the platter of bread down.

Jonathan's phone pinged as I was scooping up the thick stew. My mouth watered at the smell. When did I last enjoy a home-cooked meal?

"Gabe isn't coming by for dinner," Jonathan said.

Rhys snorted. "Yeah. I bet it's 'cause he's still sulking."

Stefan chuckled. "I'm sure he'll love to hear you say that."

I looked between them. "Gabe? That's your oldest brother, right? Why is he sulking?" I hoped I wasn't being too forward.

"Yep, he's our oldest," Jonathan replied, voice filled with pride.

"Yeah, oldest *baby.*" Rhys rolled his eyes before looking at me. "He's a little ticked off because of the whole changing the logo and update thing."

My eyes widened. "Because of me?"

Jonathan patted my arm where he sat to my left. I looked his way and saw him shooting Rhys a look before meeting my eyes. "Actually, he's upset because that one over there"—he used his chin to gesture at Rhys—"only gave him so much of a heads-up."

"Thirty minutes, to be exact," Stefan supplied.

"Yeah, because Gabe takes forever to—"

Stefan interrupted Rhys before he could finish his sentence. "He takes care of everything and everyone." His look to Rhys was pointed, and for some reason, it felt like I was missing something.

"What they're trying to say," Jonathan chimed in, "is once he sees your amazing work, he'll forgive his brother for springing everything on him."

I knew that Jonathan was trying to make me feel

better, but suddenly, a pit formed in my belly. I knew I could do good work, but it felt like more pressure knowing that the person in charge hadn't wanted to hire me in the first place.

My appetite disappeared, and I couldn't help wondering if that feeling of rightness had been premature. What if this Gabe person was just counting down the moments until he could give me the boot?

A hand wrapped around my wrist, and I looked up to find Rhys beside me. He'd moved from where he sat next to Stefan at the round table.

"Trust me, I know Gabe will love your work. The moment I thought of the rebrand, I knew you'd be perfect. You're so talented, Kian." Rhys's voice was firm.

"My son is right," Stefan said, and I turned to look his way. "Rhys may be impulsive, but he's usually spot on."

"I didn't just hire you 'cause you're my best friend and lost your papa." Rhys' voice was kind.

And I swallowed because the thought had crossed my mind.

"I know you can do this, Kee. Trust me, Gabe would have vetoed this if he didn't trust me to make the best decision for the company, even with only thirty minutes' notice."

"He's right," Stefan agreed.

The words helped, but it still meant I had something to prove. But I could do this. I had to. Because now that I was here, I really didn't want to leave.

I swore to myself I would give this my all...not that I wouldn't before. But I *would* win Gabe over if it was the last thing I did.

4

GABE

"Is he there today?" I asked my assistant, Bailey.

I didn't have to see her to know she was rolling her eyes. "No, I believe he won't be in today."

"Are you sure?" I asked.

"Yes," she replied, "For Urs's sake, don't you think you're being just a little bit stubborn about this whole thing? He's actually quite lovely if you just gave him a chance—"

"Bailey." I made sure my lack of patience was clear in my tone. We'd been friends since we were kids, and I honestly couldn't have done the job of running our company and the den without her, but right now…I just was not in the mood.

Bailey was an alpha like me, and she made sure all the *T's* were crossed and *I's* dotted, while I took care of the big picture. I trusted her implicitly. But this definitely was not one of those times I needed a lecture.

"Just make sure he's not coming in today, okay? I have a few things I need to take care of."

"I know you do, and I don't see how one omega is—"

"Bailey," I snapped, my patience wearing thin. If she knew how much it took for me not to be there. To see him.

I sighed and pushed my hands through my hair. "Just do this for me. Please."

She managed a put-upon sigh like I'd asked her to rob a bank. "Fine. I'll call Rhys, but you know he's going to bitch at me about you, right?"

"Yeah. Yeah. I know, I owe you. How about a trip to the spa?"

"Gabriel Hallbjørn, are you trying to bribe me? Because it's working. Rebecca and I would love a trip to the spa, and if you really wanted to make it up to me, you'd watch your godson for the day."

I chuckled. "But of course. How could I do any less?"

"This is why you're the best boss and an even better friend; I won't hold the fact that you're being a bullheaded ass about the sweet new guy against you...this time. Because my wonderful wife would kick my ass if I mess up a spa and kid-free day for her, so this time, I will do your dirty work."

I snorted, but the thought entered my head about my godson and our child—mine and Kian's—playing together. Would they be best friends like Bailey and I were?

I sucked in a breath at the thought of my mate large with our child.

Gods! Staying away from him was killing me.

I'd managed to avoid my mate for three whole days, and my bear was none too pleased. Actually, he was pissed and sulking. Not that I was doing much better.

Just knowing Kian was my mate made everything better... *Even though you're too chickenshit to do anything about it.*

Still, even without the mating bond, it was like I was attuned to him; I could always tell when he walked into the building, even without laying eyes on him. And I hated that I couldn't... *No one is stopping you.* I ignored that voice. The asshole had no sense.

Every single part of my body took notice when Kian was close by. Some parts more than others.

But what the hell was I supposed to do, though? He was human. What if I scared him off? What if he lost his shit when he found out what we were?

Sure, there were a couple of human mates in the den, but that was from my grandparents' generation. One from my parents' generation, too, I believed. One thing was certain, though—no one in recent times had mated with a human. I wasn't even sure what the rules were for it.

So why don't you just ask? Clearly, it was allowed. And I knew I could ask my dad. *So why haven't you?* The possibility of being told I couldn't mate with my mate was slim. *What's holding you back?* Right now, it was simply a case of meeting my mate officially, not some bogus rule about keeping away from humans.

Bullshit. You don't believe there is one.

"Mates trumped everything else…" So why didn't that helpful reminder have me rushing over to my brother's house and meeting Kian officially for the first time?

Maybe introducing myself…asking him out on a date. Or was that too forward? Fuck, I didn't even know where to start.

Did I blurt out what I was…what we were before even asking him out?

Pacing back and forth in your kitchen won't give you any answers.

"Kian." I wrapped my tongue around his name. It was a beautiful name.

Gods, I really wanted to know everything about him. I wanted to wrap him up in my arms and make sure that he knew everything would be okay. He'd just lost his papa. I found myself wishing I'd been with him as he'd gone through all that. That he'd known he didn't have to go through it alone.

I sighed. None of this was doing me any good. And I really needed to get to work. Even though Kian had been given an office to work from in the main building, I was glad that he preferred working from home. So far, he'd only been at the office once to meet everyone. That was the day I'd suddenly had to go to the factory for a meeting.

Rhys was pissed at me. He said I wasn't giving Kian a chance...if he only knew. But I really wasn't in the mood to explain myself to anyone, least of all my baby brother. He wouldn't get my caution. Like with most things, he'd expect me to dive in headfirst and hope for the best.

Which may be a good thing. It would mean you wouldn't be drinking coffee by yourself this morning. Also, I wouldn't have woken up alone... I just wouldn't be alone anymore.

Making sure the business was successful had been my sole focus for a long time, so dating hadn't really been a priority. Gods, there'd been a lot of lonely nights.

I sighed, walked over to the sink, and poured out my unfinished coffee. I was already anxious enough. The last thing I needed was caffeine.

My phone dinged, and I looked at the screen.

Bailey: He's not here, you big baby.

I snorted but let out a breath. I would go to work and figure out the rest later. *Yeah, if you can focus.* I hadn't really gotten as much done as I usually did. But who could blame me?

I hurried over to my study and grabbed my laptop

since I'd been working from it the last couple of days, then headed out.

Once I got in the car, the phone began to ring. The display said it was Rhys. I groaned. I really didn't need another long rant from my brother, but I couldn't ignore Rhys's call.

"Rhys?" I hope he heard the tone of my voice and took note.

"Oh, thank Urs, you answered. Kian needs help. His car overheated or something on the way off the ranch, and he's stranded. Can you go get him, please? I'm at the factory today." My brother sounded upset, and I rolled my eyes at the theatrics.

"Seriously, this is beneath you, Rhys. I know you want me to meet Kian, but honestly—"

"Stop, Gabe, I'm serious. You're the last person I would have called, but Papa and Daddy are not home, and Austin is in a meeting, and Hunter is at the station, and Graham is over here." He sighed. Shit. He was serious—my mate was in trouble.

"I'm on my way. Don't worry. I'll go get him."

He's safe. He's fine, I repeated to myself over and over again, trying not to push down on the accelerator. He was still on our land, after all. Nothing would happen to him.

Even though it took less than seven minutes to get there, when I finally pulled up, I blew out my breath. I didn't bother turning off the car. I simply opened the door and jumped out.

"Kian! Kian!" I called, hurrying to the opened hood of the car, but he was nowhere to be found.

"Kian?" Fuck, where was he?

"Hello?" I turned around at the sound of his timid voice and came face to face with my mate standing with the door between us.

"Hi," he said, "Are you... I mean, you're Gabe?"

I nodded. Fuck, I couldn't take my eyes off him. Kian was beautiful. That was the only way to describe him. From his stunning steel-blue eyes that seemed to be even more startling with the dark, sweeping lashes that matched his head of dark hair. He was perfection.

"I'm Gabe." Damn, why did my throat feel so dry?

"I'm so sorry to be a bother, but there was like smoke coming out of the engine, and I don't even know if AAA comes out here? Is there AAA this far out? Or is there like a guy? I wasn't sure. So I called Rhys, but he's at the factory today. I was working, but then I thought I would go grocery shopping." His eyes widened. "I wasn't slacking off or anything. It's just sometimes getting out and doing something mundane helps bring the ideas to the forefront. You know?"

Kian lowered his head and kicked his feet, and all I could think was how adorable he was.

"I didn't think you were slacking off," I reassured him. "Besides, we don't expect you to work every hour of the day. I'm not at all artistic, but sometimes ideas come to me at the most random times. I swear I figure out most of my best solutions in the shower."

His head flew up, and his mouth formed an *O*, which of course made me focus on his delicious, full pink lips that were just a little too wide for his face, but that made him even more attractive to me.

And maybe it was wrong to think this way, but I loved our height difference. I could just imagine his body tucked up against mine as we slept.

Kian would fit so perfectly.

Our eyes met, and when his swept down my body, I watched as his cheeks pinked, and I couldn't help smiling.

That was a good sign. My mate might be attracted to me.

The image of us in bed was so clear. That lean, smaller body pressed up against mine. My eyes traveled down his body, taking in the polo shirt and shorts he wore. His legs were lightly toned and hairless. Fuck!

I could imagine all that smooth skin against my hair-roughened one.

"Do you know what's wrong with your car?" I asked, moving back towards the hood because if he kept looking at me the way he was…I would pull him into my arms and taste those gorgeous lips.

Kian moved, and then he was beside me. It took everything I had not to react. "No idea. I just bought it. Not brand-new, though, but they said it was all good, and it doesn't even have that many miles on it." Kian sighed. "Do you think they cheated me? The lady was really sweet."

I smiled at that because, of course, my mate thought a car saleswoman was sweet. I just met him, and I could already tell he saw the best in people, and there and then I promised he would never lose that. I would protect him always.

"I'm sure she was, but I bet it's just because you did the long drive down." I allowed myself to look at him and saw him nibbling on his lips. FUCK! This was why I'd stayed away. Being close to him and not being able to touch him, claim him, was torture.

"Oh, that's a good point. It was a really long drive. At least it got me here before dying, right?"

I shuddered at the thought of him stranded somewhere and said a thank you to Urs for looking out for my mate. Getting him to me in one piece.

I faced Kian. "How about I take you on your errands and call someone to get the car?"

"What?" He shook his head. "You don't have to, really. I can walk back home, and if you give me the number, I'll arrange for them to pick it up."

I should have taken him up on his offer, but I found I didn't want to... I couldn't stay away now that I'd actually met him. Not that me or my bear actually wanted to.

"Nonsense." I shut the hood and turned so I was facing him. "I insist. You're a guest here."

Kian's head tilted to the side, and he studied me. "Aren't you Rhys's brother that's refused to meet me?"

My mouth fell open at his words, I hadn't expected

him to say that, but then my lips twitched. I couldn't help it. I laughed. Until I saw that Kian's hands were on his hips, and he definitely didn't seem amused.

I loved the fact that my mate had just called me out. He was strong and would definitely not let me get away with much. I was looking forward to it.

"I'm sorry. I'm sorry." I put my hands up. "I wasn't laughing at you. It's just—I didn't expect that."

He raised those arched brows. The left one had a little scar, and I wanted to trace it and ask him how he got it.

"You didn't expect me to call you out on being a jerk?" he asked.

I clamped my lips together, trying not to laugh. I refused to hurt my mate's feelings.

"I guess I didn't," I agreed.

Those blue eyes sparkled, and the corners of his lips actually lifted. "At least you admit you were being a jerk. I'm really good at my job, you know."

"I don't doubt that," I acknowledged. "I was being a stubborn, set-in-his-ways jerk."

That warranted a full-blown smile, and fuck, it made him even more stunning, if that was even possible.

"I'm sorry," I said.

He looked taken aback by the apology.

"Why does it surprise you that I would apologize?" I asked. "I was wrong not to at least welcome you to the ranch and the company."

Kian's shoulders lifted and dropped. "I guess because you don't have to. It's your company...your land..." His voice trailed off.

"Yeah, but my brother showed me your work, and you are very good. I should have at least given you the chance to prove yourself."

Even though it wasn't the reason I'd been avoiding him, I didn't want my mate to think I was the kind of man that didn't apologize when he was wrong. Besides, thinking about it, I couldn't imagine how worried he'd been.

"I assure you, it wasn't because of you." I felt the need to reassure him of that... Okay, so maybe it was because of him, but just not the way he thought.

Before Kian could reply, though, his phone rang. He looked at the screen. "It's Rhys," he said.

I nodded, not surprised that my brother called. I knew, like Kian, he thought I was being a difficult ass. His words. He was probably calling to check up on my treatment of his friend.

He needn't have worried. Kian couldn't be in safer hands.

"Yeah, he's here," Kian said.

I heard my brother say, "Good, Gabe will sort everything out."

He looked back at me, and I smiled gently.

"All right, I'll see you when you get home," Kian said. And hearing him call a house that wasn't mine home... I didn't like it.

He finally hung up and walked over to me. "Thank you," he said.

I tried not to grin like a lunatic "Does that mean you'll let me take you into town and get your car sorted?" I checked.

He nodded. "Yes, please."

"I would be very happy to." I felt like I was on top of the world. It was something small, but my bear and I loved being able to cater to our mate in this way.

"I'll just grab my things." Kian sidled over to the passenger side and opened the door. He grabbed a messenger bag and slung it over his chest before shutting the door and coming over to me.

"Here." He held out his hand, and I opened my palm, and the key fob was dropped in it.

"Thank you," he said. And he looked relieved.

"Anytime," I said softly, holding his gaze.

Those high cheekbones were slashed with color, and he looked away. "I hope I'm not completely messing up your day."

"Not at all." I put my hand at the nape of his back because I needed to, and he shivered. I felt like I'd just been branded with that simple touch.

I couldn't contain the rumbling growl that came from deep within my chest. *Mate! Mine!*

My bear reminded me it was actually *Ours*. My bear was pushing me to carry our mate to our house and claim him. But my human side knew I couldn't do that.

Neither of us said a word as I led him to the passenger side of my Land Rover and helped him in.

"Thank you," he murmured but wouldn't look at me. I watched as he pulled his seatbelt, and his hand trembled slightly.

It shouldn't, but it made me smile. I closed the door and made my way around. Maybe it was wrong to be so happy, but I was thrilled knowing I affected my mate.

I was fucking ecstatic. Because he was driving me crazy. At least it wasn't one-sided.

IT WAS quiet in the car at first, and I watched my mate out of the corner of my eyes. He was sitting straight up, his hand in his lap.

"So how are you liking Asheville so far?" I asked. "Can you see yourself making this your home permanently?"

Kian slowly turned my way. And I found myself holding my breath. Asheville was my home. Not only that, it was my responsibility. If my mate didn't like it here, I couldn't exactly pick up and leave.

But you would, a voice said.

"I've not seen much of it," Kian replied, "But what I saw when I drove up was pretty cool. You have a windmill." He sounded fascinated by this.

I smiled and nodded. "Yeah, my couple of greats—"

He chuckled. "Couple of greats?"

I nodded and glanced at him quickly before facing the road again. "Yeah, great-great-great—I'm never quite sure."

I saw him nod, and his lips curved in a smile. "I see how that can get confusing. Okay, carry on," he prompted.

I grinned. "Right, so my great-great times something parents settled here in the late 1800s. And by the time they were building, they missed home, so even though we have pieces of our new land here, you can see hints of the old country too."

"And that would be Denmark, right?" he asked.

"Close." I nodded. "A small village in Denmark bordered by Germany."

He turned to face me. "Wow, that's pretty cool knowing exactly where you're from. I think we're English, but I really couldn't tell you anything else. Have you ever been?"

I nodded. "Not in the last few years, but yeah, we still have family up there."

"Wow, Europe, I've always wanted to go," he sighed.

"Maybe I could take you someday," I suggested, then froze when I realized what I'd just said.

The car was silent for what felt like an age but was probably no more than a minute, if that. "I mean, if you ever decided to go, I could tell you cool places to visit."

If I wasn't driving, I would have slapped myself for that. He probably thought I was a weirdo now. *Normal people don't offer to fly to Europe with people they just met, Gabriel.*

"Oh, thank you," he murmured in a small voice.

Fuck, I'd blown it. He would probably make an excuse and run from me once we got into town.

The silence stretched until I finally began pointing out the sights as I drove. "That's the Junior-Senior High School, to your left." I pointed at the newly renovated building that was just off Main Street. "The building was just renovated two years ago. We even have a swimming pool now for the kids." Kian didn't reply, but I could tell he was listening. "Next to it is the elementary school. All our kids go to school in town. We also have a really good daycare center. A movie theater and a spa…" I blathered on since it seemed I'd scared my mate by suggesting we go on vacation twenty minutes or so after meeting him.

This was why I'd needed to come up with a plan. So I didn't act like a complete idiot.

Kian *mmm'd* at everything but didn't actually speak again, and since I didn't know what else to say, I kept pointing out places until we finally pulled into the parking lot of the large supermarket in town. It wasn't quite on Main Street, but you could walk over in less than five minutes.

"I'm sure you can find whatever you're looking for here." I came to a stop right at the front of the store, not wanting to park and presume I was invited.

He didn't jump out of the car immediately, which I thanked the gods for. So I took a shot.

"If you'd like some company, maybe someone to hold your basket while you shop—"

Kian turned to face me and smiled. "Don't you have to get to work?"

That wasn't a no.

"It's your first time off the ranch. I wouldn't feel right just dropping you off and leaving you to it."

Kian seemed to study me. I wasn't sure what he was looking for, but I held his gaze. Finally, a small smile appeared on his lips, and he inclined his head.

"Thank you. I'd really appreciate it," he said in a soft voice.

I tried not to punch the air triumphantly. He might not have known it yet, but spending any amount of time with him was my pleasure.

I put the car in drive and found a parking spot pretty quickly. I got out of the car and walked over to his side to find him already out.

Even though I really wanted to slip my hands into his and hold on to him, declaring him mine, I simply said, "Ready?" He nodded and fell into step beside me.

"I can't believe you guys have a Cubs here," he said.

"Lemme guess, you thought small town, so we'd have a small mom-and-pop grocery place?"

"Well—" He nodded. "Yeah."

I laughed. "I'm glad we can surprise."

"You definitely can," he murmured. It wasn't said loud enough for me to hear, but of course I did.

But did he mean me or the town? Was it a good thing that we could surprise?

He didn't know this of course, but you would find a Cubs in most shifter towns since it was shifter-owned. I'd always found it amusing they'd called it Cubs since baby cats weren't cubs and it was owned by cat shifters. You couldn't really call them a pride since they varied in species. Cubs catered to shifters and stocked a lot of shifter-owned companies. They'd been one of the first to put the Crazy Bear Products in their stores.

Of course, this wasn't a widely known fact, but my mate would soon be in the know. I hoped.

"Cart or basket?" I asked.

"Cart, I guess. Rhys doesn't keep much in the house."

Snorting, I nodded. "Yeah, because he eats at our parents' most nights."

"I know, and Jonathan and Stefan have been so welcoming, but I don't want to put them out."

My mate was so thoughtful. Still, I felt the need to reassure him. "Trust me, they're very used to having us over most nights. You're no trouble."

"Thank you," Kian said.

I grabbed the cart before looking over at him, "But let me guess—you still prefer having everything you need at home."

He shrugged but nodded. "I like cooking too.

Maybe I could invite them over to say thank you. You know for having me, welcoming me to their home... being so kind."

"I'm sure they would love that." And if I had anything to say about it, I would be there too.

Now that I'd met my mate, the thought of not spending as much time with him as possible wasn't okay with me.

Everything I learned about him made me want to know more.

I followed Kian around the store and watched as he meticulously went through the list he'd made on his phone.

Of course, everyone who saw me at the store stopped to say hello, and they all looked at Kian with curiosity. If I had to bet, the news would be around town shortly. It wasn't often I ventured into town during the work day unless it was to inspect one of the factories or I had meetings with new supermarkets or markets wanting to stock our products. So I could just imagine what the wagging tongues would say.

By the time we'd gone through the whole store, the cart was full. Finally, Kian stopped and looked at me. "I think that's it," he said.

I chuckled. "You sure? There might be some shelves you've not cleared out yet," I teased.

He looked at the cart, then back at me. "I may have gone a little overboard." His shoulder lifted, then dropped. "But Rhys won't let me pay rent or any of the bills, so I figured this was a good way to help out."

Yeah. The more I knew, the more I liked. He wasn't someone that took advantage of his friends. That said a lot about a person.

"I'm sure Rhys will appreciate it," I reassured him.

He shot me a megawatt smile. "You think? I figured since I work from home more often than not, I could make dinner for us. Did you know he has a Crock-Pot, and it's still in the box? I could pop something in and have it cooking all day. His kitchen is amazing. And my room is huge. I wouldn't feel right not contributing in some way, you know?"

Kian sounded so excited, and with every word he spoke, I may have slotted my house in the picture. Him working from the home office that was his. There was room in my house to convert one into a studio or whatever he needed. Coming home after work to dinner. Sitting down with my mate curled up against me watching a movie.

I could see it all so clearly. And I wanted it more than I wanted my next breath.

When we got to the till, I pushed the cart up to it and began unloading it for him. Kian was standing so close as he helped too, and all I could do was breathe in his scent.

Great Urs, he smelled good. I wanted to lick every inch of him.

Don't go there. Don't go there.

The last thing Kian needs is seeing you sporting wood right now. What would you say? The smell of fresh bread makes me hard?

Nope, that was the last thing I needed, for my mate to think of me as some sort of weirdo that got erections at inappropriate times.

Once we were done unloading the cart, I straightened, and thank Urs that there was no boner in sight.

"Hey, Mr. Hal—"

"What did I tell you about calling me that? It's Gabe, okay?"

"Sorry, old habits." Naomi's smile was apologetic, but she added, "Wow, we never get you out here."

I recognized her, of course, like I did almost every member of my den. I made it a point to do so.

"Hi, Naomi, how are you? How's school?" I asked.

"Great. But we're done for the summer. I can't thank you enough for your help," she said.

I smiled. "We're all very proud. You're the one that did all the work."

"Well, I still only managed a partial scholarship, so without you, I wouldn't have been able to start immediately," she said. "Thank you so much, Mister—I mean Gabe."

"I know you'll make us proud," I said. She was studying to be a nurse and midwife, and we always needed those around here. Even though we could use human hospitals, we made sure ours was always fully staffed with doctors that specialized in both omega and female obstetrics. We also had a surgeon and a family medicine doctor.

I looked at my mate and saw confusion written all over his face, and I felt bad. I couldn't exactly say the den had scholarship for kids that wanted to go to college or trade schools and had maintained their grades.

"Naomi's parents are friends of my parents," I explained to Kian, hating to make him feel left out. Hating to lie even more. Although, it wasn't technically a lie. Still, it didn't feel good. I wanted to share everything with him.

"Ohhh, and you—" He looked between her and me. "Wow…that's amazing. I don't know many people that would help pay for college, even for a friend's kid."

Naomi's eyes had narrowed at my explanation. Then I watched as she discreetly scented Kian. Her eyes popped wide, and her mouth formed an O.

I sighed. Yup, the grapevine would definitely be buzzing.

When Naomi was done scanning, and Kian put the last bag in the cart, I slipped out my card and handed it to her while Kian made sure everything was organized to his satisfaction.

She smiled and put it in the card reader. She held it out for my pin right as Kian asked, "How much is that, please?"

The moment he saw I was paying, he hurried to my

side and nudged me. "No, you can't pay." He looked at Naomi. "Cancel that, please."

She shook her head, and I could see she was fighting a smile. "I'm sorry. It's already gone through." She cut the receipt and was about to hand it to him, but I snatched it before he could get his hands on it, before he tried paying me back.

"This is my treat," I said.

Kian folded his hands, and a determined look was on his face. "No. I told you Rhys won't even let me help out. If you pay for this, then I'm not contributing."

I could swear he was about to stamp his feet.

"Well, how about you treat me to lunch? I'll even let you pay," I said.

I could tell Naomi was paying close attention even though she pretended not to. Luckily, seeing as it was a Tuesday, there weren't that many people in the store, so we weren't holding anyone up.

Kian's mouth opened and closed, and he looked over at Naomi, then back at me.

"Are you... You're asking me—"

"To lunch," I finished for him. I didn't think saying a date was the way to go right now. My mate was not ready for that.

"Lunch," he mouthed.

I waited as he seemed to consider it. Gods, please let him say yes.

"The cold stuff will melt. And the meat could go

bad." Did Kian sound relieved at coming up with that reason?

"Hmm, well, I can fix that. Come on." I grabbed the cart, knowing he would follow. I didn't think everyone needed to know more about our business. I didn't stop until we were back at the car, and I popped the trunk and began unloading. I could feel Kian's presence beside me, but he didn't speak, simply began helping load up the trunk. When we were done and I straightened and faced him, it took a second, but Kian finally looked up at me.

"So lunch," I said. "Your treat?"

"If we have to go back to the ranch, there'll be no point coming back to town, and we need to get these in the fridge and freezer." He nodded at the groceries.

Since he didn't actually say no, I took it to mean he didn't mind having lunch with me.

"I'll take that as a yes?" I pulled my phone out and held it so he could see. He still didn't say no, and I could see in his eyes that he was confused by his reaction.

"If that's the only way you'll let me contribute," Kian said softly. Our gazes held for a moment, and I let myself get lost in those gorgeous eyes. He looked away first and whispered, "Someone is on the line."

"Huh?" I asked, confused.

"Your phone. Someone answered." He nodded at my hand.

"Oh, right." I lifted it to my ear. "Bay, do me a favor

—send someone over to pick up the Land Rover and bring a replacement for me. There's groceries in the trunk. Please have them put away at Rhys's. We'll be at Holly's."

"And what, pray tell, has you lingering in town when there's work waiting on your desk?" There was amusement in Bailey's voice, and suspicion.

"Bailey," I growled.

"You know I find it interesting that you avoid the office because of our lovely newest staff member, but then suddenly, you seem to be taking the day off to spend time with him." She clucked her tongue. "Yes. It's all very interesting."

"Baileyyy." I drew out her name in warning, but the problem with someone knowing you as long as she had was they really weren't scared of you.

"You know if I was a nosy sort, I would wonder. I would wonder if maybe the reason you were avoiding our new human"—she emphasized the word— "coworker had something to do with the fact he is your ma—"

"Bailey," I snapped before she could say the word.

"It's all very interesting, you know, but of course I will have a car sent over while I ponder just how interesting things are..."

Was it possible to hate the word *interesting*? I sighed because I knew I was in for an inquisition in the very near future.

When I finally hung up, my mate's eyes were on me.

"If you have to get back to work, I understand," he said, nibbling on his bottom lips nervously.

Fuck, did he know what he did to me?

"I don't have to be anywhere but at lunch," I assured him. "With you," I added for good measure.

I could swear a small smile appeared on his lips.

I led my mate back to the passenger side and opened the door for him. When he was seated and belted, I closed the door and walked over to my side. Before entering the car, I drew in a breath and told my bear, and myself, not to fuck this up for us.

Since it was just past three p.m., I found myself hoping Holly's wouldn't be packed at this time.

The café was one of my favorites places to eat when I came into town, and for some reason, it was one of the first places I thought to share with my mate.

Also, I knew that I wouldn't run into one of my brothers here. Rhys was at the factory or more likely the brewery since he'd been working on expanding it with Graham. Graham was probably at the café or his office at the factory where their Crazy Bear baked goods were made and packaged. Of all my brothers, I had to worry the least about Graham. He was way too busy. Even Papa had complained.

Austin would be at his office in town hall and Hunter at the station or the diner since that was where his mate was—not that my brother was having much luck there. So I should be good on having to explain anything…at least until I got home.

Not that I didn't want to claim Kian to anyone I could.

"Gabe, good to see you, son." Lars's booming voice welcomed us as we walked into Holly's.

"Lars, how's things?" I asked, smiling at the older man I'd known all my life.

"Can't complain," he said. "Peter should be home any day now."

I grinned because I knew how worried Lars had been when his only son Peter had left town, but he'd finally gotten his degree in accounting and was coming home.

"We can't wait to have him at the office," I said. "Top of his class."

The old bear puffed up like the proud papa he was. "Now all he has to do is find a mate and give me some grandcubs."

My eyes widened, and I looked over at Kian, but he didn't seem to be paying attention. Instead, he was looking around the café.

"I thought it would be all quaint inside too." My mate's voice had me focusing on him.

I smiled and nodded at the plates on the exposed brick walls. "What about the blue plates and all the framed pictures?"

"I think it's cool, like it's very old meets new." I led

him over to a table tucked in the corner, so we couldn't be seen by passersby. "The whole town is."

"Thank you," I said. I was proud of my home. We never forgot where we came from, but we also made sure to evolve with the times.

"I love all the half-timbered storefronts. It's very European." He shrugged. "At least I imagine it is. I've never been. Were those storks I saw on the roof?"

I chuckled and nodded. "Yup. They're plastic, but we see them as a sign of good luck."

I tried not to think of what storks also meant, but it was too late. The picture of Kian heavy with our child flashed in my head, and I wanted it to be real so badly.

I picked up the menus that lay on the side of the table and handed one to him.

"Thank you," Kian said and shot me a grateful smile. "What's good here?" he asked, opening the menu.

"Everything," I replied, looking through the menu even though I already knew what I would be getting.

"That's why you're my favorite, Gabe." I grinned and looked up to find Holly, Lars's mate. She was a tall, thin woman with hair so pale it was almost white. It had been that way for as long as I could remember.

"Holly, good to see you," I greeted her.

"Gabe." She smiled at me before focusing all her attention on Kian. She looked between us, a calculating glint in her eye. Yeah, I was in for an inquisition in the very near future.

"And who might you be? I don't believe we've met," she said. "I'm Holly." She held her hand out to him.

Kian's smile was shy as he took her hand. "Kian. I'm new in town. It's lovely to meet you."

She looked between us again and grinned. "Lovely to meet you, Kian. I have a feeling I'll be seeing more of you around these parts."

"He's Rhys's friend, just moved here to work at the office." No one asked me, and I didn't know why I felt the need to explain. But I saw the amusement in Holly's eyes.

"Right, well, you order whatever you want, even from the breakfast menu. We'll be happy to make it. Just give us a shout when you're ready to order."

With that and one more knowing look, she left.

"She's very nice," Kian said.

"Yeah," I agreed, even while knowing she was probably back there calling Gods knows who.

"You see anything you like?" I asked.

My mate licked his lips, and my pants definitely began feeling a little tighter.

"I've always wanted to try crepes, with like Nutella or something in it. I've seen videos on Instagram, but I never knew where to go," he said. "But I should have a sensible lunch, right?"

"Who says? I think I'll have the same. We can both be a little wild today," I teased.

He shot me a smile that had my heart racing.

"Nutella crepes then, please, and hot chocolate?" It was phrased as a question.

"Sounds perfect," I agreed.

"Coming right up," Lars called out.

Kian's eyes widened, and he leaned forward. "How did he hear that?"

I sighed because I hated lying to my mate, and without telling him what we were, there were too many things that could only be explained by a lie.

Still, I sighed and replied, "Acoustics."

"Ooh. Cool," Kian said, nodding.

My bear huffed. Neither of us liked lying to our mate.

"So tell me about yourself," I said. "How did you end up a graphic and web designer?"

Kian picked up his fork and began twirling it as he spoke. "I always liked to draw, but I didn't think I was ever going to be an artist, but my papa—" His voice caught on the word, and I leaned forward and covered his hand that rested on the table.

"I am so sorry for your loss, Kian. I can't imagine having to go through that without my brothers." I squeezed his hand softly. "It just shows how strong you are."

He laughed, but there was no joy in the sound. "Can I tell you a secret?" His voice was barely above a whisper.

"Always, Kian, you can always tell me anything." I

made sure to hold his gaze so he knew I meant every word.

He ducked his head and blew out a breath. But I didn't push him, and I didn't let go of his hand.

"I don't feel strong," he whispered. "Some days, it's all I can do not to scream at how unfair it is." His voice broke, and I wanted to scoop him up in my arms and tell him it would all be okay. Protect him from the pain.

"Most people would have folded after going through what you did, but you didn't let it break you. Look at you—you're here, making a new life. I bet your papa would be so proud of you."

Kian sniffed. "I don't even know why I'm telling you all of this. We just met. I'm being silly." He sat back in his chair and pulled his hand out of mine.

I felt the loss, more than I should since my mate was still sitting in front of me.

"What you feel is never silly, and I will always be here if you want to talk, Kian."

He looked up and met my eyes, and I held his gaze steadily, needing him to see I wasn't just saying it for the sake of saying it. I meant it from the depth of my soul.

Kian looked away and, in a small voice, said, "I thought you didn't even like me."

Great Urs, help me. I need to fix this.

5

KIAN

TODAY WAS THE DAY, AND I WAS ABSOLUTELY GOING TO puke before I got to do this presentation.

Butterflies had taken up residence in my belly, and no matter how many breathing exercises I tried, they refused to budge.

The problem was I wasn't even sure what made me more nervous. Presenting my designs or presenting them to Gabe.

I couldn't seem to get a read on the alpha. At first, I'd been certain he couldn't stand me and was just biding his time till he could fire me. And the whole "refusing to meet me" kind of supported my theory.

But then we'd met, and I couldn't stop thinking about the day I'd spent with him. It was six days later, and I'd gone from not laying eyes on the man to finding him everywhere I turned.

Maybe because you suddenly started spending more time in the main office.

I did prefer working from home, but for some reason... *You know the reason.* I ignored that voice. I was simply being more friendly meeting my new neighbors. That was all. It had nothing to do with six foot six inches of broad, handsome, and somewhat grumpy alpha.

That was my story, and I was sticking to it.

I refused to focus on how attentive Gabe had been at lunch. How I'd told him things I hadn't admitted to anyone else—not even to Rhys.

How I wanted to just rest against that broad chest and have those muscular arms hold me tight and never let go.

None of that matters, Kian. You're here to do a job, not ogle your new boss. Not to mention he's your best friend's brother.

I still wasn't sure which part worried me more. The fact that Gabe was my boss or the fact he was Rhys's brother. *Rhys, who's your only friend in the world. Your support system when you need him. Basically, all the family you have left.*

It wasn't like I planned to do anything...and even if I did, it really did not matter. It wasn't like anything would happen. *He probably doesn't even think of you like that.* But there were times when I'd thought maybe I'd caught a look when Gabe suddenly showed up at Rhys's for dinner.

Maybe he spends time at his brother's house. It could have absolutely nothing to do with you.

I growled, covering my face with my hands. This wasn't doing me any good. I'd done a job. I would present it like the professional I was.

And you will not think about what Gabe looks like under that perfectly tailored shirt and slacks. You most definitely will not think about rubbing up on all those muscles.

I was so screwed. *Yeah, and all banging your forehead on the table is doing is giving you a headache.*

The door to my office opened. "How did I know you would be in here spinning out?" I felt Rhys stand beside me, but I didn't look up.

"What if he hates it, and I have to find another job?" I whispered. My heart raced at the thought of having to leave Asheville. It was only ten days since I'd gotten here, but the thought of having to go back to Philadelphia held no appeal. Or worse yet, somewhere I'd never been with people I didn't know.

Rhys rubbed his hands up and down my back. "He won't. Besides, these are just early sketches to see what you have in mind. It may take a few tries to get it perfect, but it doesn't even matter. This is your home." My friend's voice was firm.

And my heartbeat slowed gradually. Maybe that was what I'd needed to hear. I knew Rhys was my friend, but this was still a business. If I fucked up, I would be fired, and I couldn't just stay in town and mooch off him.

Rhys clucked his tongue. "There you go again, worrying."

"How do you know?" I sighed. "Maybe it's too soon. Why didn't you stop me from setting this meeting? You should have looked at the sketches when I tried showing them to you."

My heart was racing again, and it took everything I had not to bring up the coffee I'd had this morning. I'd known better than to eat breakfast.

The last thing I needed was a Mia Thermopolis moment from *Princess Diaries*. Puking on my boss—and crush. I ignored that helpful addition; clearly, my brain didn't know what priorities were.

"First of all," Rhys began, still rubbing my back gently, "if you need more days, take them. I'll cancel the meeting. I'll be honest and say I thought you would take some time off before jumping into work, but Papa said maybe this was your way of dealing."

I grunted. It was as close to a yes as I could get right now. Work was a distraction. I knew if I let myself, the grief would pull me under, and that wasn't what Papa had wanted for me. He'd said I should be happy and find someone that made me smile every single day just by being them. He said he was going to be with Daddy now. And as much as I hated to admit it, there was a little relief in there. Not because he was gone, but because he wasn't in pain anymore. Seeing how gaunt my papa, who'd been full of life, had gotten... I swallowed down a sob.

"You know what, maybe we should reschedule. Your heart sounds like it's about to hop out of your chest." Rhys sounded concerned. "Breath, Kee. Everything will be fine, and to answer your question from earlier, I know how talented you are, and I didn't want there to be any doubt. I know I'll be blown away when I see it, and I don't need to see it beforehand to practice a reaction. But again, if you're not ready…"

I growled loudly and sat up. "I'm ready." I nodded. "Yeah. Yeah, I can do this."

"Of course you can, Kee," Rhys said, and I looked up at him and couldn't help smiling. He always had faith in me. I didn't know why, but he did.

"Why do you believe in me so much?" I asked, my voice sounding a little needy even to my ears. I shook my head. "Actually, never mind."

"Look at me," Rhys instructed. My best friend didn't repeat himself; he simply waited.

I drew in a deep breath and slowly let it out before turning in my chair and looking up at Rhys. He cupped my cheek and smiled down at me gently. "Because you don't know just how amazing you are. And until you do, I'll be right here telling you."

I leaned my forehead on his belly, and Rhys slipped his hand into my hair like he used to do when I would lay with my head on his thigh. "Love you," I whispered.

"Love you too," he replied, and even without looking at him, I heard the smile in his voice.

I wouldn't let Rhys down. He had faith in me. Put me forward to his family. It was up to me to make sure he never regretted it.

Before I could change my mind, I blurted, "I'm ready."

Rhys's hand stopped moving in my hair. "Are you sure? You know this doesn't have to happen today."

I shook my head. "No. No. I can do this. I'm ready."

Rhys studied me for a moment before inclining his head. "All right, come on then. Let's do it."

I picked up my laptop and iPad. Straightening, I asked Rhys, "Everything is set up, right?"

He nodded. "Yeah, you just have to connect the HDMI cable to your laptop, and you're good to go."

"Good. Good," I muttered, wiping my suddenly wet hands on my pants, then froze. Shit, that was just what I needed—a wet spot on my slacks. Everyone would focus on it during the presentation.

When I looked down, everything was fine. Black slacks. I'd forgotten I'd worn black slacks.

"Seriously, you look like you're gonna keel over. We really don't have to do this today. The meeting is—"

"Now," I finished for him. I was doing this. I could do this. *Just don't look in Gabe's eyes.* I cursed that reminder. "Come on," I prompted Rhys, who was studying me like he could see into my mind. I sincerely hoped not. The last thing I needed was him teasing me about having a thing for his brother.

Which I didn't.

WE WALKED side by side to Gabe's office, which I actually hadn't been in yet. Rhys didn't bother knocking; he simply opened the door and walked in.

"I can always count on you to knock." Gabe's tone was dry, but I couldn't help smiling because even with the hint of irritation in his voice, there was affection.

"Well, you were expecting us, so if we caught you in a compromising position, that would be your fault," Rhys said, and he lowered himself to the two-seater leather couch in one corner of the office instead of one of the two chairs in front of the large wooden table Gabe sat behind.

"Rhys." Gabe sighed, and there was a wealth of exasperation in that one word. The alpha got on his feet, and like it always did, it hit me just how everything he was...commanding, broad, big... *Nope, don't even go there.*

I refused to think of how his arms would feel wrapped around me or the fact that he could definitely lift me up like I weighed nothing.

And the white shirt he wore seemed to draw more attention to those muscled arms of his. Until meeting the man, I never knew I had a thing for tall, broad, leanly muscled men. The differences between him and Danny were almost exaggerated.

A hand on my shoulder jolted me out of my thoughts, and I looked up to find Rhys standing in front of me. "You okay?" he asked in a whisper.

Fuck! Just what I needed—drooling over my boss and forgetting where I was. *Way to aim for employee of the month, Kian.*

"I'm ready," I said.

"Do you think you'll want to step away from the door and get set up?" Rhys's voice was soft like he was addressing a cornered animal. I groaned internally. This was definitely not the impression I was trying to make.

"Of course." I stepped away from the door and almost ran straight into Gabe. His hand went to my left shoulder, and I felt the touch to my soul. My eyes flew up to meet his, and he was looking at where our bodies were joined.

Fuck, why did I have to go and have thoughts about our bodies being joined?

If I wasn't already swoony for him, Gabe asked in a soft voice, "Are you okay?"

I found I had to swallow, and even then, my throat felt too tight to try and force anything out.

"Fine." I nodded and took a step back. Having him so close was not good for my already fragile equilibrium. The alpha made me feel things I never had, and it scared the crap out of me and left me off-kilter, trying to decide if I wanted to burrow into his body or run as far and fast as my legs could carry me.

Gabe took a step back and inclined his head. "Good, well, ready when you are." He walked back to the couch, and I was finally able to breathe, but then my senses were overwhelmed with what could only be his scent.

Dammit, I should have so taken Rhys up on postponing.

I nodded and felt Rhys's hand on my back to lead me towards the flatscreen TV on a rolling stand that had clearly been moved in here for this exact purpose.

Rhys helped me get all set up before whispering in my ear. "You got this." Then he left me to put my password in.

I didn't immediately open up the logo or the mockup for the new website. Instead, I turned to face Rhys and Gabe, even though I made sure I didn't actually look the alpha in the eye.

"I didn't want to completely change everything that makes the brand so recognizable, but I thought it could do with a little sharper branding. And the heart of the company, from what I've seen, is quality and, more importantly, this land that seems to be so essential to your family."

I spied a look at Gabe, but I honestly couldn't read him. But I knew he was listening. He seemed like the kind of person that didn't miss a thing.

Okay, so step one done. Now show them the design.

I went on my browser and opened the new page for

the website. And held my breath before speaking. "I went around and took pictures of the land. I know the animals aren't raised here anymore, but Rhys said it's very similar to your uncle's where you get your cows and stuff from." I tried not to panic when Gabe's face remained impassive. "As you can see, I kept the blue and yellow, which are existing colors."

No one spoke, but I saw a small thumbs-up from Rhys. As good as it felt, he wasn't the one I was trying to impress. I really wanted Gabe to like me... I meant it...my work. And it wasn't just because he was my boss, but focusing on that right now wouldn't do me any good.

I turned and opened the Photoshop app with the logo. I didn't speak immediately. I let them take it in and said a prayer that the silence wasn't because they hated it so much and they just weren't sure how to tell me.

I turned to look at the logo, even though I knew it by heart. It was a roaring bear lunging through a fence, the type/font of the ranch name, and a ranch-type scene under that in monochrome lavender. I'd kept all the original colors, just added some oomph to it.

I looked at Rhys, and he wore a smile. Although I couldn't really tell what the smile meant, but when he met my gaze, he gave me two mini thumbs-up.

"How about you go first," he prompted Gabe.

Gabe didn't speak immediately, and his face was

inscrutable. The butterflies in my belly were definitely trying to get out, and my heart was pounding so fast you would think I'd just run a marathon with no training.

"Why does the bear look so angry?" was the first question out of Gabe's mouth.

I looked over at Rhys, and he looked as taken aback as I was.

"Because it's a bear," I said slowly.

"Yeah, but why do we even need a bear on the logo? I think CBR and Crazy Bear Ranch beneath it now is simple, and it works, right?" He looked at Rhys for support, but my friend simply stared at his brother. "The website looks nice, though," he tacked on, "but maybe we hold off so we don't shock our current clients."

Rhys jumped on his feet and put his hands on his waist. "I knew you would do this. I bet you didn't even give it a chance. I love what Kian came up with it. It's simple and elegant and just cool. Plus, if these are just the first mock-ups, imagine how good it'll be when it's the final." Rhys paced back and forth. "I knew it. I told Daddy and Papa you would do this." He spun around and faced me. "Don't listen to him, Kee. You did an awesome job, and I love it, and I'm sure if I showed Papa and Daddy, they would too. And since they're still on the board—"

Gabe growled and got on his feet. "Enough!" He

didn't raise his voice, but I felt the power behind the word down to my toes. "It's my job to take care of the company now, Rhys, of everything. I am in charge." He punctuated each word.

Rhys's hands curled into fists, but he didn't speak, even though it looked like he had something to say. "I said I will consider it, and that's exactly what I will do."

His words were firm, and Rhys looked like he wanted to scream, but for some reason, he didn't say a word.

Gabe turned to me. "The website does need to be rebuilt. Clients have mentioned freezing and such, so maybe start there, but don't change too much."

"Are your freakin' serious?" Rhys blurted. "This isn't what we talked about. I thought you brought me on because you appreciated my input. Apparently not." Rhys seemed to draw in a deep breath before putting both hands on my shoulder. "I'll see you at home. I need a run." He didn't look at Gabe again as he left the office, and then it was just the two of us.

I went over to get my laptop and tablet. This hadn't gone anything like I'd imagined. There was a part of me that had imagined Gabe praising me. I didn't expect to cause a fight between the brothers.

I could feel Gabe's presence, but the man didn't speak. I turned to leave, and he whispered, "I'm sorry."

I turned around slowly, and the alpha actually looked like a kicked puppy. Why did I feel the need to comfort this man? He'd just basically shut down my ideas. Hell, I had no idea where I stood with my job.

"It's your company. You get to make the decisions on what you think is best," I said. Then I hurried out of the room before I did something crazy like throw my arms around him.

6

GABE

I'D BEEN CURSING MYSELF SIX WAYS TO SUNDAY SINCE the meeting with my mate. I'd also gone back to avoiding him. I didn't want to see the sadness in his eyes that I'd clearly caused. There was no doubt in my mind that he was talented, but the truth was I couldn't just change over ninety years of history. Our business was doing well, very well. Wasn't it my job to make sure I protected that, kept it going?

So why couldn't I get Kian's defeated eyes out of my mind? His shoulders had slumped, and he'd looked like a kid who'd just been told Santa wasn't real for the first time.

My bear had growled at me for that, then gone silent. The asshole was actually giving me the silent treatment.

All my bear and I'd wanted when Kian had stood in my office looking like he was about to break down was to comfort him, but I knew right then, my touch would not have been welcomed. Not that I could blame him.

I wanted to go over to Rhys's and see Kian... explain. But what was there to say, really?

"Hey, I know I didn't approve your designs, but how do you feel about going on a date with me?"

That would go just swimmingly. *Not.*

And my brother would definitely pour gasoline on that fire, calling me an ass and every other inventive name he could come up with. Even Bailey had called me an idiot.

I sighed, pushing my hands through my already messy hair. This wasn't how it was meant to go. I was supposed to meet my mate. He was supposed to know who I was...what I was... He would then agree to be mine, and we would spend a couple of weeks locked away learning everything about each other. Mind. Body. Soul.

On the heels of that thought, I knew without a doubt—whoever that mate was, he wasn't Kian, and I wanted Kian.

Instead, here I was about to spend yet another night alone when my mate was two doors down. And this time, I couldn't pop over for dinner. I had a feeling the door would be slammed in my face if I did.

I blew out a breath and rubbed the back of my neck. Yeah, thinking wasn't helping. I needed a run. When I let my bear out, things were less complicated. I was still me, but a lot of the human worries were dulled for a while.

I wasn't sure that would work this time since my bear and I wanted Kian with staggering ferocity.

My cock stirred, thinking about my mate's trim body in his slacks and shirt.

My hand and I had gotten very reacquainted since I'd scented my mate, but even that was getting hollow. I didn't want to jerk off over him. I wanted to lick and suck every inch of him before sliding my cock into his welcoming heat. I wanted to mark him and hold him close so that when he was covered in my scent, there would never be any doubt he was mine. Great Urs, I wanted more than a solo jerk session. I needed Kian in my home, in my life, in my bed where he belonged.

With that depressing thought, I walked out back to my patio, and I quickly took my clothes off and left them on the chairs before walking down the stairs and letting the change come over me. Like always, it was smooth. My bear and I had always been in tune with each other. Although he wasn't too pleased with me at the moment because of the way I was dealing with our mate.

I ambled through my garden out into the night, the sharp vision of my bear guiding me even in the dark. I loved this land. My great-great-grandparents—I always forgot how many greats—had come here from Europe and settled here. They'd built Asheville as a safe place for shifters. All kinds of shifters. Back then in Europe, the mating between two species hadn't really been accepted, and as the story went, the two of them, a wolf and a bear, had decided to leave. Start their life elsewhere.

Which was why my cousins, who lived not too far away from here, were wolves.

I let my bear roam for a while, enjoying the freedom he gave me. I wouldn't get lost, no matter how far I went in this form. I would always find my way home.

I stopped at one of the smaller ponds on the property and lay down there. Even being in this form didn't stop the yearning, and for the first time, I was fighting my bear, trying to stop him from doing what he wanted.

Sighing, I lay down still in bearskin and watched the stars. All the while wondering what Kian was up to right at this moment.

I wasn't sure how much time passed—it couldn't have been that long—but being out here wasn't doing much to help. I didn't have any more clarity, and my mind wasn't any clearer, so I got up and headed home.

"Eeeeeep." The sound had me freezing.

"Please don't eat me." My mate stood frozen on the deck of Rhys's home, and he looked like he was about to pee his pants.

Shit, how hadn't I noticed that I'd headed to Rhys's? If I'd been paying attention, I'd have scented Kian before my bear and I scared the heck out of him.

I shook my head and backed away a little.

Kian's head tilted to the side, and I could read the confusion on his face. I knew he couldn't hear me in this form, but I hoped the mate bond that existed between us would help him see that he wasn't in danger with me.

I sat and put a paw up. Kian looked confused for a second, but then his body relaxed slightly.

"I should run, but you seem nice," Kian said.

I nodded, at least as best I could like this.

"But bears can't be nice. I forget, am I supposed to stay super still or make myself really big?" Even as he spoke, he didn't move a muscle.

I chuckled at that. But honestly, though, I needed to teach my mate that a flight response sometimes was the way to go. Not that I would ever let anything happen to him.

"Are you hungry?" Kian asked. "I'm sure we have honey in the house."

I chuckled, but it came out as a snuffling sound.

"I don't know if bears actually like honey. Maybe that's just Winnie the Pooh." Kian shook his head. "Obviously, you don't know who that is. You probably don't even understand me."

I laughed and nodded and batted a paw at him.

"Or maybe you do?" Kian looked confused. "You

don't look so scary. But I don't think I should come any closer."

I lay down so I didn't terrify him.

"Awww, you don't look so scary at all."

I nodded, my big head moving up and down.

"I wonder, do bears feel like teddy bears?" Kian mused, taking a step towards me.

I tried to make myself as non-threatening as possible. My bear was dying to meet our mate in this form.

7

KIAN

EVERY INSTINCT IN MY BODY WAS TELLING ME TO RUN the other way, so why was I moving towards a wild animal?

When I was a couple of steps away, the bear turned to me, and I could swear he smiled.

Yeah, probably because you just made yourself dinner.

"I think maybe I should go back inside." I backed away, but he growled, and I froze.

Yeah, this is it. This is how you die, Kian. Your obituary will read "He was too stupid to run from a bear. He actually approached."

When the bear stood, I gulped. Holy fuck, he was huge.

"Please don't eat me. Please." *Fuckity fuck damn.* I should scream…or run or something, but my legs had suddenly stopped working.

When he, or maybe it was a she—yeah, because

that's what's important right now—moved towards me, I stood very still, even as my whole body broke out in a cold sweat.

When the bear stopped right in front of me and put his huge head against my belly, I gulped. A voice in my head said, "All the better to gut you."

It nudged me, and I gulped. Gosh, it was hard to swallow. Then the bear nudged my hand.

My head tilted to the side. "You want me to pet you?"

The bear nodded, its large head moving up and down.

Okay, Kian. You can do this. Pet the bear and then run like hell. Maybe this was a fever dream? Maybe I was in a hospital bed somewhere, and they were trying to save me, and my brain was having a Disney moment. Although I wasn't sure there was any Disney fairytale with a bear. Was Goldilocks Disney?

Yup, definitely a fever dream.

I put my hand on the large head in front of me, and the bear let out what I could swear was a pleased moan.

I pushed my hand through the fur, and it nuzzled into my belly.

Was this really happening?

The fur was actually soft and felt nice to run my hands through. "Soft," I murmured.

It kind of hit me that this wasn't a Pomeranian or Beagle. I was stroking a bear, so I gingerly took a step back.

The bear did too and stared at me, and I looked at him, and there was something familiar about it.

If I was thinking that, then I was clearly losing it. I backed away. The bear didn't move, simply stared at me. I didn't take my eyes off it till I was on deck. "I'll throw something to you." When I finally got to the door, I went into the house.

The bear watched me, not moving, and I felt bad leaving him there.

I DIDN'T BREATHE EASILY until I was back in the house. I stood with my back to the screen door while trying to slow my racing heart, but it seemed to be doing its best attempt to jump out of my chest.

But there was something about the bear... *Is that why you're about to take an apex predator honey?*

I knew it was crazy, but I could swear that it understood what I was saying...but that was crazy, right? If I hadn't stayed frozen, it would probably have ripped my face off. So why did it feel like the bear had been trying to say I was safe?

I snorted at myself. *Bears can't say diddly, Kian.*

But that didn't feel quite right, though. It almost felt like he'd been laughing at me at some point, like he understood me...

HA! You're definitely getting too much fresh mountain air. After all the pollution in the city, it's clearly making you loopy. Bears did not communicate with humans. It was sheer luck I hadn't died out there tonight.

Did that mean I was stuck on crazy since I headed to the kitchen and the pantry to grab the honey? As I opened the door to the beautifully arranged room, I couldn't help sighing in pleasure.

This pantry made me happy with its white shelves on all three walls and the pullout basket drawers beneath the wall facing the door.

It was all organized, and it was a label maker lover like me's dream. That was something Rhys and I had in common. For a second, I wondered if I would ever have a home of my own with my partner and a super arranged pantry. I could see it now. I would work from home because I had my own office there with a crib in it... I would make batches of homemade baby food for my little one and store it in the fridge.

I would walk in and find my husband and our son or daughter with their faces covered in chocolate chips after eating too many of the cookies I'd baked.

Shaking off that thought, I grabbed the honey and hurried back the way I'd come, halting at the door to the deck.

"This is crazy." *I should just go up to bed.* I sighed. I couldn't. There was something about the bear that seemed almost familiar... Of course, technically, I knew it was impossible. I'd never seen another bear before, at least not outside of the zoo.

You're losing your mind, Kian. Completely over the cliff

looney. Next thing, you'll see Wile E. Coyote trying to blow up something or pull some other shenanigan on The Roadrunner.

Still, I opened the screen door since the actual door was left open, which was crazy because if the bear had charged, the damn screen would have been no match.

I'd thought it was completely ridiculous when Rhys said he rarely locked his front door, but now here I was possibly about to make myself dinner to a hungry bear.

The moment I stepped outside, I knew without even having to look that I was once again alone. The bear was gone. Why this knowledge was followed by a pang of disappointment was a mystery to me.

My rational brain was relieved, but there was a part of me that insisted I'd never been in any danger. *Yeah, the part that clearly needs to be in bed 'cause you've obviously been hallucinating.*

That voice that said I'd never been in danger didn't shut up even as I slipped under my covers. Maybe this had all been a dream?

As I turned off the light by my bed, I knew I was wide awake, and I'd just been face-to-face with a real bear.

The freak-out was sure to follow.

8

GABE

I'D SLEPT SOUNDLY AFTER COMING HOME. I DIDN'T KNOW what it was, but my bear had been so happy meeting our mate, and he hadn't been scared of us... Well, he had, but only like eighty percent of the time.

I tried to focus on the memory of his hands in my fur. My head on his belly. I wanted him to do that in this form.

I could still smell that clean cinnamon and vanilla scent, it was like walking into the house when an apple pie just came out of the oven, and my cock thickened. I wrapped my hand around my already half-hard cock, and just thinking about my beautiful mate had me at attention.

I stroked my dick and groaned. Gods, all I could see was my mate, that lean, lithe body stripped and ready for my attention. I shut my eyes and let myself get lost in the fantasy. My lips around his nipple, biting down lightly until he let out a moan and ground his hard cock against my leg, seeking some relief.

I imagined sliding my thick cock into that welcoming heat, and I picked up my pace just thinking about that body made just for welcoming me. Joined completely in every way. His legs wrapped around my waist as he begged me to move.

Those gorgeous blue eyes dark with lust and heat and love… The thought had goosebumps breaking out on my body.

"Fuck yes," I cried. Gods, I wanted it more than my next breath. Kian under me, on top of me. Riding my cock, taking his pleasure from my body.

He would beg me to go harder and faster, and I would flip us over and pound into his hole. Staking my claim on him.

"Mine," I growled to my mate, increasing the pace of my hand on my dick.

"Yours," he breathed.

Dream Kian moaned, lifting his hips to meet every thrust. His fingers leaving marks on my back. Claiming me in his own way.

Fuck, I was so close. My mate's hole clenched around my dick as he begged me to claim him.

"Fuck, yes!" I groaned as my orgasm crashed into me and my dick spurted over my fist.

When my cock twitched for the last time and the last trickle seeped out of my slit, I leaned against the shower wall and asked the Gods to show me how I could claim my mate. Because these solo sessions were no longer enough.

I finished the rest of my shower quickly and got out. I wanted to lay eyes on my mate. I wondered if he would actually show up at the office today... Was it too soon to turn up for breakfast, or did I need to make myself scarce a little longer? I really didn't want to.

Sighing, I went to my walk-in and grabbed a shirt and slacks. I tried not to look at the empty right side of the closet. It was sad. I'd cleared it out the moment I'd scented Kian. The house was all but ready for him to move in.

Would he find that presumptuous? Humans didn't really move in after knowing each other for a couple of days. Although it had been twelve days... That was a good amount of time.

Where you've spent most of the time mooning over him from afar.

My phone pinged, and I welcomed the distraction. I got dressed quickly and headed to my room to grab it.

Rhys had texted me. This should be good.

> **Rhys:** Just because you're an ass doesn't mean you gotta skip breakfast. Kian is nicer than me.

I snorted at that. My baby brother, ever the snarky one. But I wasn't about to turn that down.

I shoved my phone in my pocket, got my shoes on, and was out of the house in less than two minutes.

I practically jogged over to Rhys but then stopped a couple of feet away from his house. Apparently, my parents were joining us for breakfast. I had a feeling this was more of an ambush by my brother.

Why was I even surprised?

Not that it was enough to keep me away from Kian.

I didn't bother knocking. I simply opened the front door and let myself in.

I drew in a deep breath, straightened my shoulders, and plastered a smile on my face.

"Papa, Dad, good morning," I said as I entered the kitchen. Apparently, my brother Austin had also been invited. I shouldn't be surprised.

"Morning, son," my papa said. I leaned down and kissed his cheek, and he looked up and patted my cheek.

"Son," my dad said. "How are you?"

"I'm good, Dad," I replied. "Austin." I nodded at my brother.

He glanced up at me and nodded but finished chewing before he said, "Big brother. How goes it?"

"It goes. You? How's City Hall?"

"Permits, planning, meetings, same ol'… You know all the wonderful things that keep the town going. You know how it goes."

I did. Austin and I worked closely together as much as we could. Asheville was both our responsibilities.

I took a seat in the only empty spot that had a place setting, and it was beside Kian.

My bear and I were very pleased by this, and I looked over at him. "Hello, Kian."

"Hi," Kian mumbled but didn't look up at me.

I didn't think my heart could hurt this much. Fuck, my mate was so mad at me he wouldn't even look my way.

I closed my eyes and drew in shallow breaths, trying not to hurl, especially since my stomach was empty. Not only that, but it would just be the icing on the cake of how to embarrass yourself in front of your mate in one easy step.

"Kian was telling us about meeting a bear." Rhys's voice broke through the whooshing sound in my ears.

I turned to face Rhys, and my brother's eyes were filled with amusement. "Tell 'im, Kee."

All eyes went to my mate, and he ducked his head. "I think maybe it was a dream," he said. "'Cause there's no way it really happened," he muttered under his breath.

I didn't like the way he sounded. Like he thought he'd hallucinated the whole thing. Great Urs, had I made Kian doubt his own mind?

"Why don't you tell us?" I prompted gently. "I'm sure you'll find believers amongst us."

"In case you hadn't noticed, we love our bears around here," my brother Austin said with a chuckle.

"There's an understatement," Rhys muttered under his breath, and I pinned him with a look. Kian didn't need to think he was being made fun of.

"Ignore my juvenile children," my papa said, giving each of us warning looks. "Tell us what happened."

Kian looked at Papa and nodded. He drew in a breath, seeming to collect himself before speaking.

"There was a bear." His voice was barely above a whisper, like he couldn't be sure if he should say it. "And he just kind of sat there, and he even let me pet him." He sounded like he wasn't sure it had actually happened.

We all exchanged looks, and I was kind of hoping one of them would say something because I sure as hell had nothing. But all eyes were on me, and my papa had a knowing look in his eyes that made me want to look away.

"I think," Papa said, "everything will become clearer in the very near future."

Kian's brow crinkled, and he looked even more confused, and I could swear he thought we were crazy for even believing him.

"Our family has a very strong connection to bears," Austin added.

"Mmmm." Rhys nodded.

"You could even say we all have our inner bears," I said.

Rhys rolled his eyes and snorted. I knew if it was up to my baby brother, he would tell Kian everything right now. But I wasn't sure my mate was ready.

Or is it you that isn't? Too scared you'll chase him away when he knows the truth.

I ignored that voice and chose to focus on the fact that Kian hadn't seemed as terrified as I'd thought he'd be.

"Can you believe I even went to get honey for him, but then he was gone when I got back?" Did he sound disappointed, or was that just wishful thinking on my part?

Rhys burst out laughing; he actually shook with it. "He went and got the bear honey—how cute is that?"

"Cuckoo, you mean." Kian's lips twitched, which I would take over him doubting himself.

Austin held out the honey on the table to Kian. "How about you give this to Gabe? I'm sure he'll appreciate it as much as any bear."

That had everyone else at the table in stitches.

Kian looked my way, and our eyes met and held. His cheeks flushed, and he lowered them again. I wasn't sure what came over me, but I leaned closer to him and whispered in his ears, "I would love honey from you anytime." I wanted to nip the sensitive skin of his lobe. I wondered if he would moan for me, but I hadn't earned that.

Kian shivered, and I could scent arousal on him, and I knew everyone else could. So when I met Papa's gaze, there was a triumphant gleam there. Like I'd just proven his suspicions right, and when he nudged my dad and they both looked at me questioningly, I looked away.

I would bet they suspected Kian was mine. They

knew me well enough to know I'd never come close to him otherwise.

And I could bet that once Rhys knew Kian was my mate, he would never let me hear the end of it. I just knew that when he would tell the story of how we met, he would make it seem like he had known all along and that was why he'd invited Kian down.

I would never hear the end of it. And knowing my little brother, he would use it to get anything he wanted.

Not like he didn't already.

9

KIAN

Okay, so this wasn't exactly my vision, but the client was always right, right?

I studied the new design one more time. It was basically the same as the old one, just crisper, with updated fonts. I literally hadn't done anything, if I was being honest.

Sighing, I shared a look with Rhys, who'd chosen to look at it this time before we showed it to Gabe.

More so now than before, I wanted to add the bear, although maybe he wouldn't be roaring.

"You're definitely going to laugh at me for saying this," I said, leaning back in my seat and looking up at Rhys, who'd been standing over me watching me put the finishing touches on.

"Try me," Rhys said.

"Okay, so I know this is completely off the walls

cray-cray, but after meeting my bear"—my cheeks heated using *my*—"I mean the bear, I feel like the logo needs it more than ever."

Rhys squeezed my shoulder, and I turned in my chair to face him. "That's not crazy," he said. "There's —" Rhys sighed. "Just trust me. It's not crazy."

I frowned. This wasn't the first time that it'd seemed like Rhys wanted to tell me something but stopped. Which was weird because you usually couldn't shut him up to save his life.

Maybe it was wishful thinking, but three days ago, after what the Hallbjǫrns had said about bears and this land, it'd felt like something was missing. Although this time maybe not a roaring bear, but roaring was right. He watched over the land and the people, fiercely protective.

Like Gabe. The thought floated into my head.

I sighed. I really needed to get rid of the bear thoughts. *And Gabe thoughts.* But that was a different matter. I was still convinced it had been a dream, but then I'd had dreams with the bear again, and I knew those were dreams.

I rubbed my temples. *Focus, Kian.*

None of that mattered if I lost my job, and the way things were going with Gabe... I ignored the flutter in my heart just thinking about him. Why did the alpha leave me feeling off-balance?

Even that whole thing about honey he'd said—I'd

felt it down to my toes. I could still remember how his warm breath had felt against my skin.

So not going there. *He was just being nice? Even you know better.* He was flirting… At least I think he was. But why a man like that would flirt with little ol' me didn't make any sense.

He was still the first guy I'd ever been attracted to from the moment I'd laid eyes on him. I'd never had that weird butterflies-in-my-belly feeling, not to mention the dry mouth. And I'd definitely always thought the whole stuttering mess was a myth.

Not that it mattered. Most times, I was sure the man didn't even like me…but then he would do something nice like send me lunch on the days he knew I was at the office or have my car fixed and returned to me running even better than when I'd bought it and there'd been no bill to speak of.

I startled at a hand on my shoulder. "Earth to Kian." Rhys's voice pulled me out of my spiral. "If you're worried about Gabe, this is exactly what he wants, so I can't see him complaining." Rhys pursed his lips. "It's just so boring." He huffed. "Whatever. Come on. Let's get this over with."

"Are you sure we don't need to make an appointment?" I asked. "I'm sure he's busy."

"Nah, we have one, technically." He held up his phone. "I told Bailey to let me know if he's in a meeting, and she's been keeping me up to date. He's free."

I nodded and stood. Gosh, I should have sprayed all over my body with antiperspirant. It would be just great if I ended up with sweat spots when Gabe saw me.

I closed my eyes and drew in a calming breath. "All right. Let's do this."

Rhys patted me on my shoulder. "You're awesome." He sang the last bit, and I couldn't help it, I smiled.

We exited my office and walked side by side to Gabe's at the door. I grabbed Rhys's hand before he could turn the knob.

He didn't speak, simply gave me a moment to collect myself. I willed my heart to beat slower, and I did my best to silence the loud voice that kept screaming *you suck* over and over again.

When I was sure I wouldn't nervous-puke or, worse, fall flat on my face at Gabe's feet, I took my hand off Rhys's.

He didn't ask me if I was okay; he simply squeezed my hand before opening the door and walking into Gabe's office.

The alpha didn't look up from what he was working on. He said, "One day, you'll open the door and see something you don't want to." His tone was dry, and there was no anger there. But the image of Gabe and me, his big body between my thighs as he thrust into me on his large wooden desk, flashed before my eyes.

My mouth might as well have been the damn

Sahara Desert, it was so dry, and I would certainly have tripped if it hadn't been for Rhys steadying me.

He gave me a quizzical look, and I knew if I gave him the sign, he would extricate me from this meeting. But since the main reason for wanting to run in the other direction was the simple fact that I wanted his brother to do dirty, sexy things to me, I figured it was best I stayed put.

I spied a look at Gabe and found his eyes on me. For a split second, I could swear he was having the same thoughts I was, but the look was gone so quickly, it probably was me projecting my feeling on him.

Gabe looked away from me to Rhys, and I felt the loss. Which was crazy...then again, that seemed to be my word of the year.

I pulled myself together and took a seat in one of the two chairs in front of Gabe's table. Rhys took the other. I'd decided against a whole presentation this time. I had the mock-ups on my iPad.

"So," Rhys spoke first, "since you're all boring and want the same—"

I jumped in, interrupting Rhys before he said something that'd put Gabe in a bad mood. "I took all your suggestions and created a new idea that keeps everything the way it was, but still updates it and makes it stand out in this competitive market."

Gabe leaned back in his seat and linked his fingers together, studying me. I tried not to make any sudden moves, and it was like he could tell because I swear his lips twitched.

"All right then. Let's have a look." He leaned forward and held his hand out. I gulped and picked up the iPad I'd placed on my lap like it was my baby and I was trying to protect it from judgment.

My hands shook as I lifted the tablet, but I stopped it and handed it over, making sure not to touch Gabe as we made the exchange. But it felt like he purposely touched my hand and even held on. I finally looked up, meeting his gaze, and it was only then that he let go.

My heart thumped in my chest, and my palms were suddenly sweaty. It took everything I had not to wipe them on my pants and even more not to stare at Gabe. This was the height of unprofessionalism. Not only that, but I'd just gotten out of a relationship; I couldn't...shouldn't want to start anything with anyone. Wasn't there even something on the grief sites that said not to date...or maybe that was AA. I had been watching *Madam Secretary* from the beginning for like the fifth time while I worked yesterday, and maybe I was like Stevie, always picking the wrong guys...

I squirmed in my seat; was it hot in here? Dammit, why couldn't I stay on task? It felt like whenever I thought about Gabe, all the oxygen got sucked out of the room. When I was in his presence, I forgot everything else.

I groaned mentally. *You soooo need to get your priorities straight. Work first.*

The silence seemed to drag, and no one spoke. I finally looked back up and saw that Gabe was studying the tablet. I couldn't help wondering which option he was on. Was that a smile?

I looked over at Rhys, and he gave me a small thumbs-up. It seemed he was seeing what I was. I finally blew out the breath I hadn't even realized I'd been holding.

So imagine my devastation when Gabe looked up at me, then over at Rhys, and said, "I'm not sure. I need to think on it."

Rhys growled, and it took me aback for a second because it sounded surprisingly animalistic. He jumped to his feet and pointed at Gabe. "You liked it. I know you did—you're just being stubborn because it was my idea."

"Rhys." The warning was clear in Gabe's voice, but my friend just kept going.

"I know you liked one of them. I was watching you. You smiled." Rhys's voice was insistent. "Kian saw it too"—he looked my way—"didn't you?"

I opened my mouth to reply, but before I could, Rhys said, "This would be great for the company, and you're just being too pigheaded to see it." Rhys snapped, "I swear, you're saying you look out for everyone, but—"

Before he could finish what he was going to say, Gabe growled, and that time, I didn't imagine it. It sounded like it was from a wild animal. "Rhys!" he roared, and there was something in his voice that had everything in me responding. At my core. It made no sense, but I wanted to... I wanted to get on my hands and knees and present my very slick hole for Gabe.

I was losing it. Who got turned on watching brothers, who I knew from the last few weeks being around them loved each other, fight?

Maybe I should leave. I was causing problems for the family. The thought made me struggle to catch my breath, like I'd been sucker-punched.

I didn't want to go. Asheville had started feeling like home. I didn't think I would like it, but going to the grocery store and being greeted by name was actually amazing. People saw me out and about and stopped to talk to me.

It was a very nice feeling. Not to mention Ga—Rhys was here.

"I'm going to get some fresh air," Gabe said before striding out of the room.

Rhys slumped back in his seat, and I knew that look on his face. He was digging his heels in.

For some reason, something inside me told me to go after Gabe.

I put my hand on Rhys's shoulder. "I'll talk to him. Maybe I'm not getting exactly what he's looking for."

Rhys sighed and patted my hand on his shoulder. "Trust me, it's not you. He's just being a stubborn-ass bear."

I managed a smile at the bear reference. Although

I wasn't sure Gabe would technically be considered a bear. I still wondered if he had a sprinkling of hair on his chest. There was something about a light dusting on a man's chest that tapered into a trail which disappeared into... *Nope. You're so not going there.*

I HAD to ask Bailey where Gabe would be after I'd gone outside and couldn't find him. And now here I was standing outside the man's house, and I couldn't seem to ring the bell. I hadn't been able to the last six or so minutes.

When the door opened, I stumbled back, but Gabe moved so quickly and steadied me.

Gabe held my gaze. The intensity in his eyes stole my breath, but then his gaze shuttered, and I felt...like I'd just lost something.

He stepped back, even going as far as putting his hands behind his back, and a fanciful thought struck me. What if he had to do that because he was trying to keep his hands off me?

Screaming *touch me please* at the top of my lungs would be...insane, right?

"Did Rhys send you?" Gabe's voice pierced my thoughts.

I shook my head. But couldn't seem to form any words.

How cliché, Kian... Does the big, handsome alpha leave you speechless?

The truth was now that I was here in front of him… I wasn't even sure what I'd planned on saying.

I cleared my throat. "I just thought maybe we could build on the branding you liked." I lifted up my iPad and opened it, then held it up so he could see, then flicked between the images, looking between him and the screen. "I thought maybe if we worked together, we could make it perfect."

Gabe didn't say anything, but those hazel-green eyes never looked at the iPad.

"I thought… I mean, I was almost certain there was one you liked?" I didn't want to look too closely at why I needed him to like my designs. It wasn't like I didn't have other clients. I'd made sure to reach out to all my clients, even the ones I'd had to let go while Papa was sick. And I'd restarted my profiles on online platforms for freelancers, and I already had several orders. But I wanted Gabe to want me.

Not want me…want my work.

Sighing, I closed my iPad cover. "Maybe this just isn't the right fit. I'm sure there are other designers out there you can hire…"

Before I could even think of where to go with my statement, I had those muscular arms wrapped around me, and I was pulled into Gabe's chest.

"I don't want anyone else." He growled the words out. "Only you." Then his lips slammed down on mine.

I was stunned for a minute, but it was like my hard drive finally booted up, and I moaned into the kiss.

I told the part of my brain that was chanting *Gabe is kissing me* over and over to shut up, and I slid my hands into the thick brown hair like I'd dreamed of doing.

His hand cupped the back of my neck as he laid claim to my mouth. The kiss was possessive, all lips and tongue and teeth. It was fucking hot and like nothing I'd ever experienced.

I should probably stop this. This isn't right. Is it?

I told my brain to fuck off. What did he know? Whatever this was, it obliterated every other kiss before it. Wiped them from my existence.

No one had ever laid claim to every part of me with just a kiss. The feel of his palm gripping the back of my neck and his arms banding around my waist, holding me to him like I weighed nothing, was incredible.

God, he smelled good. How did he smell so damn good?

His mouth hypnotized me. Was that even possible? If this was a dream, I didn't want to wake up.

My fingers felt the light beard he always seemed to sport, and it wasn't spiky. It was actually soft.

I moaned when he turned me so my back was against the wall of the house, and he ground his hard— oh my days—just like every other part of him that, too, was huge.

My hole clenched, and I wanted to feel that cock sliding inside my body.

My dick leaked in my jeans, and I knew my hole would be slick, ready to take him.

Gabe nibbled on my bottom lip before dipping his tongue back in, and all I could do was whimper. It wasn't enough.

Gabe made a sound that was half moan, half groan into my mouth, and I drank it in. No one had ever made me feel this wanted.

The most incredible kiss of my life suddenly stopped. Gabe looked into my eyes, and his were so dark they could be black. I saw lust and need there. And I wanted everything the look promised, but then I was suddenly back on my feet, and it was a miracle I didn't puddle on the ground at his feet.

He stepped back, and in a voice that seemed to be dragged from his soul, he said, "You have no idea…" He pushed his hands through his hair. "You don't leave. Swear to me you won't leave."

I nodded like a marionette on a string. And the next thing I knew, he was gone.

Did he realize he'd just run from his own house?

Sighing, I let myself slide against the wall till my ass hit the ground. I wasn't sure what had just happened. But it had to happen again.

Minutes ticked by, and then it dawned on me that I'd dropped my iPad during all that. Dammit, was there even an Apple Store in a ten-mile radius?

Maybe I would come to, and this would be an elaborate hallucination…or a fever dream.

I sure hoped not.

Also, was I meant to wait here till he came back? I banged my head gently against the wall. Fuck, this Alpha was giving me whiplash. So why did I want to run towards him and not in the other direction?

10

GABE

THAT HADN'T HAPPENED TO ME IN A LONG TIME. IN fact, I couldn't remember the last time I'd lost control of my bear. Maybe when I was six or seven. But kissing my mate had brought me so close. My bear was extremely pleased after that kiss. We wanted more. Finally having Kian in my arms. It was everything I'd wanted it to be. Kian had responded to me so well, his body ready and willing. All my bear had wanted was to claim him, and Gods, I wanted it too, but...

Yeah, even I was getting sick of coming up with reasons why I couldn't.

I'd gotten as far away from my house as I could before letting my bear take over, but that led to a fight about returning to Kian, and now here I was, back at the house I'd grown up in. Thankfully, there were still sweatpants stashed in the laundry room, or I'd be screwed.

I kicked my feet and got the porch swing moving again and sighed. I wasn't even sure why I'd come here if I was being honest.

Hearing Kian say he might leave… It'd felt like my heart was being ripped out of my chest. Even though I hadn't claimed him yet, I knew he was close by. Even without being mated, the mate bond had already begun forming, and I could feel when he was close by. But if he left…

For the first time in my life, I knew I wouldn't be able to put Asheville or my den first. I would go after him… I would follow him wherever he went.

I didn't know what to do, and I felt like an ass because the logos he'd come up with were great, but what would happen if I approved one? There would suddenly be a clock on his stay here.

I needed more time. *No, what you need is a damn plan.*

I groaned when I heard a vehicle approaching. I wasn't in the mood to—Gods, was I being punished?

"He's gonna think I'm a stalker," my mate said.

"Trust me, son, he won't," my papa reassured my mate. And he was right… I kinda liked that Kian had tracked me down… Not that I'd even known I wanted him to.

Why wasn't I surprised? Even though Papa hadn't come out and asked me anything, I knew he knew.

I looked up at his approach, and dammit, I wanted him back in my arms. He stopped at the bottom of the stairs and nibbled on his bottom lip. Growling *mine* wasn't the way to go, even though every fiber of my being screamed it. His lips were mine to nibble on. Every part of him was mine to cherish.

I waited for him to speak first even though I didn't know what I was hoping to hear.

"Your papa said this is where you grew up," Kian said.

Of all the things I expected out of his mouth, that certainly hadn't made the list. I was waiting for him to ask me why on earth I'd kissed him.

He looked up and studied the house for a moment. In a soft voice, Kian said, "It looks like it has a lot of happy memories."

That made me smile because he wasn't wrong. Growing up had been amazing with all my siblings. Austin and I were thick as thieves.

"Must be nice having so many siblings." I could hear the sadness in his voice, and I wanted to comfort him. Let him know that my brothers were his now, and so were my parents.

"Yeah, very loud and rowdy," I said, chuckling. "I don't think Papa kept anything breakable in the house for years."

Kian's gorgeous lips curved. "I can imagine, with all of you running through the house. I wouldn't have either."

An image came to me of Kian running after our

kids in the backyard of our house while I put together a swing set for our little ones.

"Do you want a big family?" I asked.

Kian smiled and nodded. "Definitely, but I wouldn't mind just one healthy kid. My parents tried for more kids, but it never really happened for them. It would be nice if my kid weren't all alone if something ever happened, though."

He didn't need to add like he was with his parents gone. "If anything happens, they'd have Rhys's kids and—"

My mouth snapped shut the moment I realized what I said.

"That would be great." Kian grinned. "Rhys's kid as my kid's best friend, just like he's mine." He met my gaze, still smiling. "I never thought of that."

If I had my way, they'd be more than just best friends—they'd be blood. Cousins. Family.

We fell into a companionable silence which Kian finally broke when he said, in a soft voice, "I don't regret it." "The kiss," he added, like I didn't know exactly what he'd meant.

I smiled. Both my bear and I were thrilled to hear that, but did it really change anything?

My bear growled, screaming at me to stop being a boneheaded idiot.

Why was it so hard to admit this to Kian? He would understand… He would, wouldn't he?

But what if he didn't? What if this was too much for

him... But was just having him close enough? Without ever telling him what he meant to me... What if one day, he met someone?

I growled, and Kian took a step towards me. For some reason, that made me happy. That side of me didn't scare him.

Because he doesn't know what it comes with. What if he knew you could turn into an almost nine-hundred-pound wild animal? That would go down swimmingly.

My bear called me a coward. Or maybe it was me calling myself a coward.

"Are you okay?" Kian had only climbed up one step, but when our gazes met, his was filled with concern.

"What? Why do you ask?"

"You growled," he pointed out. "Rhys does the same thing when he's frustrated or upset... It's weird. I don't know why I never noticed it before." He shrugged. "But anyway, you growled."

"I guess it's a family trait," I said and leaned back, folding my arms before I did exactly what I wanted to do, which was the same thing I always wanted... although *want* didn't seem to capture what I was feeling.

Hold Kian. Love Kian.

"I don't regret it either," I said.

He climbed up another step. But before he could take the next one, I said, "But it doesn't change anything." I sighed, rubbing my eyes. "We can't do this."

Kian tripped as he took the next step but caught

himself before falling.

"Oh," he whispered.

Fuck, I couldn't take the devastated and confused look on his face. I watched Kian fold in on himself, and hurting him made me want to puke.

"I want to. You have no idea how much I want to." Maybe it was unfair of me, saying that, but I needed him to know.

"Is it because of—"

"No." I didn't bother waiting to see what he came up with. I couldn't bear to hear him talk down about himself when it was my shit that was messing this up.

There was a part of me that tried to tell myself Urs wouldn't send me someone that would betray my family or me. But one slip, and that was it. One thing every shifter the world over agreed on was humans could never know our secret. We saw how they either vilified, crucified, or exploited anything or anyone that was considered different. We would end up, best-case scenario, as sideshow freak entertainment or worse, science experiments.

I couldn't risk that. Even as I thought it, it rang hollow. Down in my soul, I knew Kian could be trusted.

Kian stared at his feet, and in a whisper, he asked, "Is it me?"

I stood up and went over to him. As much as I wanted to touch him, I didn't. I wasn't sure I would be able to stop if I started.

"You're perfect." I needed him to never doubt that. "There's just things you don't know... I can't explain."

"Try," Kian insisted. "I think there's something here." His shoulders lifted and dropped. "I know it's new, and we don't know each other very well, but...I've never felt like this before. If it's Rhys, I could ask him if he's okay with us first."

I could hear my mate's heart racing, and I knew how much it had taken for him to say all that.

"If it's because I work for you, once you approve the files, technically, I wouldn't. I have other clients." He nibbled on his lips, and I couldn't help it. I reached out and brushed the abused lip.

"I wish it was that simple." I sighed.

"Maybe we could go back to that café...on a date?" My mate's whole face was red, and even though I should say no, I couldn't. I would take whatever time I could with my mate. It was selfish. But my bear and I were weak.

"Yes," I blurted before I could let common sense take over. "We have to walk back to the house. I didn't bring a car with me."

"Your dad drove up in another car while your papa brought me," Kian admitted. "They left one for us, for when you dropped me back."

"Of course they did." I should have known my parents couldn't help meddling. I was still surprised they hadn't shown up at my house.

We walked side by side down the stairs, our hands so close but not really touching.

Over and over again, my bear repeated, *Mate. Ours. Perfect.*

"How would you feel about takeout and a movie?" I asked, refusing to even think about it. Just one night... "At my place," I tacked on.

Kian didn't reply immediately, and I was about to take it back when he whispered, "That sounds perfect."

I KNEW it was a bad idea, inviting my mate to my house, but I honestly couldn't get me or my bear to care at the moment. We wanted our mate in our house. We wanted him in our space. His scent filling it till it could never be wiped away.

So I threw caution to the wind as I opened the front door for him. The moment he set foot in the house, my bear sighed his pleasure.

Our mate was home.

"Welcome to my home," I said.

Kian smiled up at me. "Thanks, it looks really pretty. I always liked this style of house."

"I'm glad." And that was an understatement. "Please come in," I encouraged, and he walked in further. "I'll just show you around."

Kian beamed up at me. I let my bear guide me and skipped most of the rooms, instead leading him to the double doors beneath the stairs. I threw the doors open. "This is the study or library, I guess."

He raised a brow. "It's empty." He walked into the room and spun around until he faced me again, looking adorably confused.

"Well, it was supposed to be." I shrugged. "But I kind of always thought it would make a good playroom for kids or something."

Kian walked around the room and nodded. "I can totally see that. Some low shelves by this wall"—he gestured to the left one—"and a cute chair and table set in this corner. They can color, oh, oh, and a toy area..." His excitement was infectious, but then he flushed, nibbling on his lips and kicking his feet. "Sorry, look at me getting a little carried away."

"No. No. It's exactly...better, even, than I could have come up with," I reassured him. It was perfect.

Kian walked out of the room. "Don't mind me. I just got excited."

Neither I nor my bear thought so. I wanted to go out and get it done.

"Think nothing of it," I told him as we walked into the family room, which was attached to the kitchen too. That had a kitchen breakfast nook, which my mate hurried over to.

"Okay, this is crazy, but I always thought it would be cool to have one of these, you know. Breakfast and dinner with the family, catching up with kids after school, maybe they do homework while I make dinner." Everything Kian said, I wanted to happen. When he turned and spied the stone fireplace, he squealed and ran over to it. "I love this. Curled under a blanket and watching a movie with…" Kian's eyes widened, and he slipped his hands into his pockets. "You have a really nice house."

Even though I wanted to show him more of it, I figured now was not the time. "I was thinking, maybe I could make something"—I took a step towards him— "or we could order if you want."

"I wouldn't want to put you out," Kian said.

"You're not," I told him. My bear wanted to provide for his mate in this most basic way. "Make yourself comfortable. I'll see what I've got."

I walked over to the kitchen and opened the fridge. I heard the chair being pulled out at the island, so I turned to find my mate with his chin resting on his hands and his eyes on me.

I smiled at him, and he blushed but smiled back at me. And neither of us seemed to want to look away. The silence stretched, and I saw his eyes flare with a need that I knew he couldn't miss in mine.

My bear… Actually, I couldn't lay all the blame on him. I wanted to put Kian over my shoulders and carry him up to my room…but instead, I drew in a deep breath and cleared my throat. "Anything you're allergic to?" I asked. My voice was husky even to my ears.

Kian swallowed and licked his lips, and I watched every move. "No," he whispered.

I nodded and forced myself to look away. "Pasta," I said. "It's easy to make…won't take long. Do you want to put on the TV? I have all the subscriptions. I'm sure we can find something to watch while I cook. Or maybe you prefer music."

I heard him move, and then the door to the fridge was pushed closed, and there he was, standing in front of me.

"Kian, please." I closed my eyes. Gods, did he know what he did to me? I wasn't even sure what I was asking him.

He took another step towards me, closing the gap between us even more. "I would really like it if you kissed me again."

I groaned. "Gods." I was only a man. My hands went around his waist, and I pulled him to me. Fuck, I wanted another taste of him.

We fit together perfectly. Like the final piece of a puzzle that had been missing under the couch and was now finally added to complete the picture.

Kian sighed into my mouth, and his arms went around my neck. I lifted him off the ground easily, needing him closer. I licked at Kian's lips, and he opened his mouth and let me in. Our tongues tangled together, becoming one. My bear was extremely pleased as well. Neither of us wanted Kian out of our arms. It was everything I'd dreamed it would be. And the way Kian responded to me, his body ready and willing…

The Gods were smiling down on me. This moment was perfect.

Of course, the annoying voice in my head pointed out it couldn't truly be perfect until he knew everything and accepted me anyway.

I growled, breaking our kiss. My arms tightened around him, and I searched his gaze as I said, "If we keep going, I won't want to stop."

Kian's lips curved, and he cupped my cheek. "Then don't."

My bear rumbled his pleasure, and Kian must have felt it because his head tilted to the side at the sound. His fingers traced my jaw, going back and forth, and I waited. His hands slipped down my neck, and I shivered. He traced my collarbone before lowering his head and nibbling on it.

"Gods," I moaned.

Kian looked back at me, eyes filled with need, the scent of his arousal thick in the air. I was barely controlling my bear.

"I prefer midnight snacks to dinner," he whispered. My brain was scrambled for a second, so I didn't immediately get what he meant. He must have known because he nibbled on my earlobe, and Gods, my cock strained against my pants. "Take me to bed, Gabe," Kian whispered.

I should say no...but I couldn't... I should wait till he knew everything about me...but I just couldn't.

11

KIAN

It was like those words from me stripped Gabe of whatever had been holding him back. He captured my lips in a kiss that stole my breath. Gabe cupped my neck in his hand and deepened the kiss. Fuck I'd never felt possession like this. It was like he was trying to write his name on my soul. Our tongues tangled as we explored each other's mouths.

When Gabe finally broke our kiss, we were both gasping for breath. I wanted to strip off all my clothes and beg him to do really naughty things to me.

"Fuck, you're perfect." His voice was deep and husky and sent shivers down my spine.

No one had ever looked at me the way he was, like they wanted to devour me whole. I'd never had such focus on me, like a predator with prey in its sights.

My heart skipped a beat. His usually hazel eyes were so dark, and I couldn't look away.

Gabe lifted me off the ground and put me on the counter, then stepped between my legs. My legs were pushed wide to accommodate his large size. I loved how big he was; it made me feel safe. He was so much bigger and stronger than I was, and fuck, it turned me on.

When did men bigger than me start doing it for me?

I'd never met a more gorgeous or stubborn man. But apparently, that was my thing too. I wrapped my arms around his neck and pulled him down for another kiss.

Gabe growled, and it vibrated against my lips, sending a tingle traveling from my mouth down to my cock. He tugged me closer, and a moan slipped from between my lips. His hands went around my waist, slipping under my T-shirt. His calloused hands on my skin were both blissfully electrifying and agonizing. I wanted him to touch me all over. He tugged my shirt and broke the kiss to pull it over my head.

Gabe stepped back, breaking our physical contact. The moment our bodies were no longer touching, a cold shiver raked down my body. It was as if I needed him. I wanted to beg him to come back, but all thought stopped the moment Gabe pulled his shirt over his head and revealed himself. "Oh, God," I whimpered. I couldn't take my eyes off him. No one should look that wow. From his broad shoulders to his perfectly sculpted abs and that trim waist. I wanted to lick every inch of him.

Gabe stepped between my legs, and I immediately wrapped my legs around his hips and trailed my hands down his chest. He shivered and growled at my touch.

"Wow," I sighed.

His hands trailed down my side, and his voice was a deep, sexy purr when he said, "You took the words right out of my mouth."

My cheeks grew hot at the sultry promise in his eyes. Gosh, I couldn't remember anyone ever looking at me the way Gabe did.

My fingers moved as if they had a mind of their own, dancing along Gabe's collarbone and down his impressive pecs. When I tweaked his nipples, he growled and nipped my lobe, sending shivers through my body. "You're playing with fire."

"Please," I whimpered.

Gabe traced down my side until he hooked his fingers in my shorts and tugged. I lifted my hips to help him pull my shorts down. My dick was hard and begging to be free.

I wrapped my hand around my dick once it was free and stroked up and down. Fuck, I was so turned on. Gabe growled and batted my hand away.

"Mine." He gripped my cock.

"Please," I begged. I just needed Gabe—I didn't care how. I just never wanted him to stop.

Gabe stroked my cock slowly like he was memorizing every line and curve. All I could do was moan and thrust into his hand.

"Perfect," Gabe whispered.

I spread my legs, trying to get him to go even lower. When Gabe flicked his nail over the sensitive head of my cock, slick gushed out of me. I gasped. My hole was wet, begging to be filled.

My legs fell as Gabe moved lower, and he looked up and held my gaze. "I've dreamed of this." His voice was ragged. His eyes closed, and his nostrils flared as he took in a big breath. A small smile curved his lips. "It's better than my dream." His eyes opened, and it was as if my heart was trying to break a rib with how hard it was pounding.

He spread my cheeks. "Gabe," I whimpered. "Please, I need you."

Gabe shuddered at my words.

He came back up, and his hot breath ghosted over my neck before his blunt teeth bit down. "You don't know what you do to me."

I felt tingles through my body, and all I could do was moan.

When Gabe's fingers teased my entrance, I thrust my hips, hoping to get him moving.

He teased my hole before pushing one inside. I gasped. "More, please."

"So hot and slick for me," Gabe said before crushing his lips to mine. I opened for him and moaned when he added a second finger.

I pushed up, but Gabe pulled out, and I dug my fingers into his back. Before I could beg again, three fingers were pushed into me, and all I could do was cry out. "Gabe. I'm ready, please. Please."

Gabe moved, and I heard a zipper. "Tell me you're sure?" The words sounded like they were dragged out of him.

"Please, Gabe."

He nipped at my neck again and nibbled. God, it was too good.

Gabe's dick pressed against my hole and slowly began to push inside. I wrapped my hands around his bicep. "Gabe," I groaned. God, the stretch was more than I'd ever felt in my life. But I wanted more—I wanted to be filled completely with this man that confused and intrigued me so completely.

"You're so beautiful," Gabe whispered. "Perfect for me."

I didn't know what we were or what this would turn out to be, but the words stirred something inside of me as Gabe pushed forward until he was fully inside me.

Our gazes met and held, and my breath hitched. I'd never been this connected to a lover before. And none of the other two people I'd been with had made me feel like their whole attention was on me. Gabe moved, and it stole my breath. My brain went blank. "So good," I cried.

Gabe grunted, "Mine."

I trembled at hearing the possession in his voice.

Gabe bit my neck, and I moaned. It felt so good. I never knew how sensitive my neck was.

I held on tight to Gabe when he lifted me off the counter and turned so my back was against the wall. He gripped my hips and began thrusting hard and fast.

Gabe hit my gland on every thrust, and I could barely catch my breath. Shock waves of pleasure were dragging me closer and closer to the edge of climax. All I could do was hold on to him as he gave my body unimaginable amounts of pleasure.

I squeezed down as he thrust, and Gabe groaned and bit down on my shoulder.

I knew I would wear his marks tomorrow, and it made me even hotter.

"Feels so good, Gabe. Harder, please." I wanted to feel him long after we were done.

"You're mine," Gabe growled. "Mine."

"Yours." I knew it was said in the heat of the moment, but I wanted it to be true.

I sighed when Gabe tightened his grip on my hips, his hot tongue licking and then nipping my neck.

"Gods, you're perfect for me, Kian," Gabe sighed.

Gabe rolled his hips, moving his cock around inside my sensitive channel. All I could do was beg. "Please, Gabe. Please."

His teeth bit down deeper on my neck, and I cried out as my body was overcome with so much pleasure my back arched and my toes curled. Gabe growled, "Mine."

Color danced in my vision, and I cried out, "Yours." I thought I was coming down from my climax, but my body reacted to Gabe as if I hadn't just had a mind-blowing orgasm.

Gabe moved inside me again, his hold tightened on my hips as he kept thrusting. I'd thought I was spent, but I felt my body reacting again.

"Kian," he groaned.

Gabe's thrusts slowed down like he was trying to drag it out. His hand circled my cock, stroking in time with his thrusts.

"I'm gonna fill you up, Kian. Mark you so everyone knows you're mine."

Why did that sound so hot?

I couldn't even think as Gabe played my body like his very own finely tuned instrument.

I felt even more stretched if that was even possible.

He nipped at the same spot on my neck again, right before he let out a loud growl and came.

I shuddered as I came again at feeling Gabe's cum filling me. I had a feeling I would never be the same again.

I rested my head against his shoulder, just trying to catch my breath. When I could finally take a breath without shuddering, I lifted my head, and I knew there was a dopey grin on my face.

"Wow—" The words immediately stalled in my throat when I saw the stricken look on Gabe's face.

My heart stopped, and my stomach rolled. Was that

confusion in his eyes? Oh my God, he looked like he regretted what we'd just done. I unwrapped my legs from his waist, and Gabe set me on my feet. My heart felt like someone was taking a saw to it. This was not how this was supposed to go.

I'd seen it in his eyes, heard it in his voice... I could swear this was something real.

"I should go," I murmured, moving around him to grab my clothes. My heart cried, *please tell me to stay.*

Of course he didn't. Instead, Gabe said, "I'm so sorry, Kian... It wasn't meant to happen like this. I didn't mean—" He shook his head. "I'm so sorry."

I backed away. I couldn't hear him say one more bad word about what we'd just shared.

"I have to go," I whispered. My body felt both hot and cold at the same time. "I need to go."

"I'll walk you home." He grabbed his shirt, and that was when I realized he hadn't even taken his pants off.

How could I have been so stupid?

"You don't have to." I tried to keep my voice even and made sure not to look at him, and I hurried into my clothes. I needed to get out of here before I burst out in tears.

"I'll walk you," Gabe insisted.

He reached out to touch me, and I flinched and moved away. "No, please." I backed away from him before turning and running out of the house. I heard him calling after me, but I didn't look back or stop until I got back to Rhys's. I shut the door and leaned against it like I thought he would try to get in, even while hoping that he would.

I slid down to the floor, resting my head on my knee. I was so stupid. Why did I let that happen? Was I so desperate I threw myself at the first alpha in my path? Had I imagined something that wasn't there?

"Kian?" Rhys's voice had me wanting to run again. Fuck, he was going to tell me to leave.

Then I would truly be all alone. God, I'd messed up everything.

"Kian, please look at me." My best friend's voice was soft, and I heard him lower himself to the ground.

"I'm sorry," I whispered. Even as tears rolled down my cheeks. "I'm so sorry, Rhys. Please don't hate me."

Rhys moved, and I felt him beside me, and he pulled me into his arms. "I could never hate you, Kee."

"You don't know what I did." I sniffed. "I can't stay. I have to go."

"Shhh," Rhys crooned. "Don't even say that. You're not going anywhere. It's not your fault. Trust me, I know. You didn't do anything wrong."

Rhys's arms around me tightened.

But I had. I should never have... God, I'd thrown myself at Gabe.

Where would I go?

12

GABE

I was a coward. A dumb, reckless coward. And worse than all that, I'd hurt my mate when that was the last thing I'd ever wanted to do.

Standing outside Rhys's house and hearing Kian crying, my bear had gone crazy, was still going crazy.

I'd wanted to break down the door separating my mate from me and lift him into my arms and tell him how perfect he was. That it was nothing he did. That I was already crazy about him.

But what would good would that do if I hadn't told him who I was?

Gods, he would never forgive me. How had I screwed this up so epically? I needed to see him. Explain. Fuck. I pushed my hands through my hair and paced back and forth.

What if my mate never spoke to me again? I'd never resented my position before, but for the first time ever, I did. Because I wasn't just putting myself on the line—it was the town, my family... It was everyone. And no matter how trustworthy I thought he was, it felt incredibly selfish to simply put myself first.

My siblings had all left for college, but I'd stayed back. Being responsible was starting to feel like a noose.

I needed fresh air; I felt like I couldn't breathe. I hurried outside. The sound of the river usually soothed me. The majestic mountain ranges in the distance that usually brought me so much peace didn't.

All I could feel was the distance between my mate and me. "Please forgive me, love." I lowered myself to the porch and hung my head.

I heard the engine of a car approaching. Didn't my family get the message that I wanted to be alone? I'd picked one of the most secluded cabins on our property, but why I expected them to take the hint was beyond me.

"This pity party looks to be in full swing," my papa said as he walked towards me.

I didn't even bother looking up. But of course it was Papa, and I would bet Dad wasn't far behind. They traveled as a pack, the two of them. As it should be when you'd found your mate.

"Ahh, I see some things haven't changed even with age," he snorted. "The silent treatment, really, Gabe?"

I loved my papa, but I just didn't have it in me right

now to respond. My brain was playing my screwup on repeat.

He sat down beside me and slung his arms around my shoulder. "Son, the world isn't ending. Things always work out the way they're supposed to; you know that, right?"

No, I really didn't. And Papa wouldn't get it. He'd met Dad when Dad had gone to visit friends in upstate New York. As the story went, Papa was working at a bar in town where Dad and his friend went to grab drinks. Papa was his server that night, and they'd scented each other, and it was a wrap. They'd gotten together immediately, and Papa moved to Montana with Pops.

"I can see you're going with defeated, which is so unlike my son. I would think that stubborn, determined streak of yours would come roaring out, especially when it came to your mate." My papa was using his disappointed voice.

I turned my head to the side slightly and met my papa's gaze.

"You think I don't know that's what he is?" Papa sounded amused. "Of course I do. I knew it from the moment I saw you around him. You didn't know it, but you did everything to stay close to him."

I grunted.

"Congratulations, son. Kian is wonderful, and I know he'll be a fantastic addition to the family."

I looked away and sighed. Yeah, that wasn't going to happen, not after I'd screwed up so badly.

He smacked me on my thigh. "Oh, quit the guilt. I know you, and I bet you're overthinking this. Okay, last night wasn't your finest hour, but we both know that was mostly your instincts at the forefront. Honestly, I'm surprised you held out that long," Papa mused. "And yes, you handled it poorly, but that's what groveling and jewelry and chocolate are for."

I snorted.

"There he is." He nudged my side. "Son, licking your wounds never solved anything, and if I know you—which I do since you shot out of me." I groaned, and he chuckled. "I knew I could make you laugh." I sighed and turned to face him.

"Gabe." Papa took my hand in his and squeezed. "I bet you've been worrying about the fact that your mate is human since the moment you met him. If I know my son, you've tied yourself up in knots telling yourself you can't break the rules."

I leaned my head on my papa's shoulder, trying to draw strength from him.

He nudged me until I looked at him again, and he took my face in his hands. "The rules are not there to punish, Gabe, neither are they there to keep mates apart."

I blew out a breath.

"I know how seriously you take your duty, son, but Urs wouldn't send you your mate just to taunt you with what you can't have. Kian has been Rhys's friend for a long time, and you've never met him because you never left the ranch. He shows up here. Don't you think there's a plan you can't see?" Papa gave me a stern look. "And that plan wasn't to show you your future and then keep you from having it."

"So what do I do?" I whispered like a little kid needing their father's advice.

"Oh, it speaks," Papa teased. "I wasn't sure." My lips curved slightly. "Well, first off, quit pushing him away. Second, you're not the first person to have a human mate."

"But this time, my mate will be the alpha-mate," I pointed out. "I'm not just sharing my secret—I'm sharing the whole town's."

"And this town knows you put it first. Your dad and I are so proud of how you take care of everything. Since you were a child, you've protected your siblings fiercely." Papa looked sad for a second. "But, Gabe, it's okay to have things for yourself. To put yourself first. Put your mate first. Besides, there's Joe and Edith in town, and Mark and Thomas, just to name a few. Joe's human, and so is Thomas. They've been mated for over twenty years each. Built a life, a family." Papa nudged me at that. "I would love some grandcubs. Hint. Hint." He waggled his brows.

I burst out laughing. "So this is all about you, right?" I teased.

"But of course. Now go get me a son-in-law so I can have some grandcubs to spoil," he teased.

"Thanks, Papa." I wrapped my arms around him for a hug. And he rubbed up and down my back.

"It'll work out, son, I promise," he crooned.

I hoped so. I really did.

I COULDN'T STOP THINKING about what Papa had said. He was right. Why hadn't I thought about speaking to someone who had been through what I was? Maybe they could help me through all the noise.

Because for some reason, I couldn't see a way through. I was always the one with the answers. Even my brothers came to me for advice, so not having them made me feel off-kilter.

I stared up at the ceiling, hoping the answers would magically appear, but Kian filled my mind. Was he okay?

It was a battle not shifting and going over to Rhys's to listen and see how he was, but maybe the best thing I could do for my mate this time was to leave him alone. Maybe that was all he needed from me. I was hurting him, and that was the last thing I ever wanted to do. But just thinking about it felt like a shredder was being taken to my insides. I just couldn't do it, and maybe that made me a selfish asshole, but I didn't want to give up my mate. I sighed. I didn't know if I was strong enough to let him go.

I looked over at the groceries Papa had brought with him. Since I'd come over shifted, I hadn't really thought about bringing anything, but right now, I wished I had some beer or, better yet, whiskey.

The door to the cabin opened, and I covered my eyes with my arm and growled, "What are you doing here? You would think leaving and hiding out at the edge of a two-thousand-acre property would give you some privacy."

"Guess thinking isn't really your thing." I didn't have to see him to know he was furious.

I knew he was baiting me; the anger rolled off him in waves. And I deserved it.

"Rhys," I sighed. "Not now, please. You can bite my head off later. Just, please... Later."

I heard him take a seat, and he blew out a breath. And I waited because I knew Rhys would say what he had to say before leaving.

"You know I came here ready to tell you what an ass you're being," Rhys sighed, "but you maybe look worse than Kian does."

It was on the tip of my tongue to ask if he was okay, but I pressed my lips together. Not only was it a silly question—I didn't deserve to know.

"Kian is—" Rhys paused, and I couldn't seem to draw in a breath as I waited for him to finish his sentence. "He's special. I just knew it from the moment we met. There was this wide-eyed innocence to him, and the truth is, my bear was drawn to him. Wanted to protect him." Rhys chuckled. "Maybe because he was always meant to be family…who knows. Fate works in mysterious ways."

I uncrossed and crossed my knees, all the while pressing down my lips, waiting for Rhys to make his point.

My brother sighed again, and I heard him mutter, "Stubborn ass," just loud enough for me to hear it, but I didn't rise to the bait.

"Kian is the least judgy person I know, like legit no judgement," Rhys continued like we were having a back-and-forth conversation. "He's the kindest, sweetest, most giving person ever." I waited for my brother to tell me I didn't deserve Kian. "And he deserves someone amazing, who will protect him and support him. Love him so completely and cherish his big heart." I shut my eyes tighter even while waiting for the body blow of my baby brother saying my mate was too good for me. *Not like you don't know that already.* "And who better than my biggest brother who I know will slay dragons for me if he had to?"

If he'd told me purple elephants had invaded the ranch, I would have been less surprised. I sat up slowly but still didn't face Rhys.

"I don't deserve him." Saying those words were like swallowing glass. "I hurt him." All I could do was sit there and hang my head in shame.

"Mmm, you did," Rhys, ever the direct one, agreed, "but only because you're being an idiot. Just tell him," Rhys said. "You know, I kinda wish I had already. Then both of you wouldn't be five seconds away from playing the heroine in a power ballad music video."

I choked out a laugh at that.

"What if I terrify him, and he runs screaming?" I whispered, sounding like a child that needed reassurance from their mother.

"He won't." There was no doubt whatsoever in Rhys's voice.

"You can't know that," I pointed out, leaning back on the chair and covering my eyes once more like it would block out my current predicament.

"On some level, he knows," Rhys said, "because Kian sure as fuck isn't stupid or reckless. There's a part of him that probably wonders. Why else would he walk up to a bear of all things? He doesn't have a death wish."

"Maybe he thought he was dreaming," I reasoned.

"I have a feeling people still run in the other direction when they see a bear in their dream," Rhys said. "You know, the only reason I never told him while we were in school was because I would hear your voice, Papa's voice, Dad's voice, your voice in my head reminding me to guard our secret. But the crazy thing was I knew if I did tell him, he would protect it too. I just didn't wanna break the rules and get anyone in trouble."

That was exactly why I hadn't told him.

"But I never stopped feeling horrible for keeping this huge secret from him. It tore me up inside," Rhys admitted.

"It's different now, though." Rhys sounded happy about this. "He's your mate. No one expects you to keep that secret from your mate unless you think fate or Great Urs fucked up…" He let his words hang there. "You have no idea how happy I am that he's yours, Gabe. He deserves someone as awesome as you. And you deserve someone as amazing as him."

Hope filled me at his words.

"So get your head out of your ass and fix this," Rhys commanded.

13

KIAN

EVEN THOUGH RHYS DIDN'T SAY WHERE HE WAS GOING, I knew. I'd seen the determined look on his face. To be honest, I was still a little surprised by how he'd reacted to Gabe and me. I pressed down on my chest and blew out a breath. Fuck, even thinking his name hurt.

Which was crazy. It was just one night. I barely knew him. So why did it feel like I'd come home and found my husband of fifteen years had walked out on me without saying a word?

We'd been so in sync. Gabe had made me feel like we were starting something new and wonderful. That thing I'd been searching for…what my parents had. But then, before I even had it in my grasp, it was gone.

I wrapped the blanket tighter around my body, but it didn't help the cold feeling that seemed to have taken hold of me.

Grow up, Kian. You had a one-night stand. No one

forced you to. Hell, you threw yourself at Gabe. So stop sitting here feeling sorry for yourself.

Of course that didn't work. And it wasn't the first time I'd said it to myself. I couldn't even meet Rhys's eyes when I'd come home last night. But my best friend hadn't cared. So that wasn't Gabe's reason for staying away. It was me.

I squeezed my eyes shut, trying not to think about it. All the while ignoring the small voice that said I was being an idiot for hoping.

I saw my phone on the table and reached for it. Rhys must have charged it and left it there. I closed my eyes and blew out a breath. *You can do this.* I unlocked my phone, pulled up the internet, and typed in Open-Move. But of course, the first box was location.

"I could go back to Philly." But that didn't feel right. It wasn't home anymore.

This is. But I ignored that voice. Staying here after… If Gabe… Staying here wasn't an option.

Although in Montana, I could still see Rhys.

Fuck, how had I screwed this up? Not only had I slept with my boss and my best friend's brother, but I'd slept my way out of a home. One I'd fallen in love with. Jon and Stefan sending out group texts telling us to come over for dinner. Or Graham popping by after work with fresh pastries. Austin and Hunter were always so nice when they saw me.

It was nice knowing that so many people cared about me.

Just not the one person I really wanted to. I didn't just want Gabe to care about me. *You want more than that...*

Okay, so Montana. I wanted to be close enough to these people that actually meant something to me.

Of course, the damn website had used my location and was showing me houses in Asheville. Was that too close?

I didn't even know. I didn't know anything anymore.

Maybe I should wait. Rhys had told me not to worry, and he'd sounded very sure of himself. And he did know Gabe better. Maybe he was just one of those people that needed time to process. But that didn't feel right, not about the decisive alpha.

But then Rhys did say I didn't know the whole story.

Maybe you're just grasping at straws.

So the cities maybe. Billings, Butte... I drew in a breath. I was going to focus on things that I could control.

I scrolled and scrolled, but I couldn't seem to find anything that worked for me. *Because you don't want to.*

It was almost two hours later when I heard the door open, and I tried not to get my hopes up, but then there was only one set of footsteps, and my heart dropped to my stomach. I was an idiot for holding out hope.

Rhys had come back by himself. I shut my eyes

tight, trying to stop the tears from forming. This was crazy. Why was I getting so emotional?

It was a couple of dates and one night. I didn't even know him that well. I shouldn't have felt the loss this much.

Rhys took a seat very close to my feet, and then he picked them up and placed them on his lap. Before he could speak, I said, "I think I found a place. It's in Missoula. It's just three hours away. So we'll still see each other. It's really nice. Actually just renovated." I grabbed my phone and went to the tab I'd kept open, maybe because I'd been expecting this, even though I'd hoped I was wrong. I turned it so Rhys could see. "Look, it's really nice. It has a back patio and a huge yard, and the kitchen was just remodeled. And it's a single-story, which I guess isn't my first choice, but it's a three-bedroom and totally in my price range...or maybe I shouldn't buy immediately. Renting might be a better idea. But three bedrooms. I can have my own office and a guest room for when you come to visit." I chewed my lips. "Maybe they'll let me rent to buy. I should look into that."

Rhys squeezed my feet, and my mouth snapped shut.

"Kee, look at me, please." He squeezed my feet again. "Please."

I closed my eyes and drew the blanket tighter around me, like it would protect me from what Rhys was about to say, before lifting my head and meeting his gaze.

"Please just give Gabe a little time," Rhys said. "He —" My friend's head dropped to the back of the couch, and he sighed. "There's an explanation for this, and I promise you Gabe hates himself for hurting you."

My shoulders lifted and dropped. "It doesn't matter. People have one-night stands." My cheeks heated even saying the words. "I guess I'm making up for lost time from college." I picked at a spot of nonexistent lint on the blanket.

"Don't call yourself that, and we both know that you wouldn't have done anything with my brother if you didn't have feelings for him."

"It doesn't matter." I shrugged. "Clearly, whatever connection I thought I felt between us was all in my head."

"No." Rhys shook his head. "Don't even think that. Trust me. It's not."

"How do you know?" Even to my ears, it sounded like I wanted Rhys to tell me it wasn't. "Why aren't you upset? I hooked up with your brother."

Rhys smiled. "I'm not upset because you and Gabe are perfect for each other. I should have seen it before."

"You're crazy." But my heart jumped at his words. He knew his brother better, so maybe he knew what was holding Gabe back. Maybe it was my imagination, but there was something Rhys wanted to say but wasn't. Although the truth was I'd felt that way for a long time. Like there was always something at the tip of his tongue. Maybe that was the same thing with Gabe. *Or maybe it's wishful thinking, Kian.*

"I'm not. I know my brother, and I guarantee—the first thing he'll do once he gets his head out of his ass is come over here and explain. Trust me, Kee. I'd never lie... I'd never lie to you about something this important," Rhys said, but there was a guilty look on his face I couldn't explain. "Come on, let's go grab something to eat, and everything will work itself out."

I'D MANAGED to hold out hope over the weekend, but it was now Tuesday, and still no Gabe. There was no clearer *I'm not into you* sign. So message received.

Even though Jonathan had stopped by yesterday while I'd hidden out and worked at home and told me not to give up on Gabe, I wasn't stupid. I could read between the lines. And no matter what his family said, Gabe himself was communicating loud and clear, and I wasn't planning on waiting to get the boot from him.

He probably wouldn't fire me, but things would slowly get awkward, and then Rhys and the rest of the family would take sides, and it wouldn't be mine. That was for damn sure.

I folded the clothes on my bed from the dresser and got the rest out of the closet. Crap, I needed to get my luggage. I sighed and left the room to go down to the garage where we'd put my suitcases when I'd moved in. I looked at the spot on the shelf where they'd been, but all my luggage was gone.

"Rhys," I sighed. I guessed he knew me very well.

I went back upstairs, and I pressed my hand to my belly as my stomach rolled again when it hit me that I was actually leaving. Truth was, I'd been feeling slightly queasy since I'd woken up, but I was chalking it up to still not knowing where I was going. And having to leave at all. But anywhere was better than here.

I still didn't know how a guy I'd only had two-and-a-half dates with affected me so much, but he did.

I sighed and sat on the bed, grabbing my phone from the bedside table. I knew Rhys would be upset, and if I could, I would have ducked out, but I refused to do that after how kind Rhys and the whole family had been.

I called Rhys, and he answered on the first ring. "Kian, are you okay? Do you need me to come home?" The worry in his voice was clear as day, and it made me feel like a nuisance. I'd basically sat on the couch the last few days binge-watching *Modern Family,* but even one of my favorite shows couldn't seem to pull me out of this.

"I'm fine, Rhys," I said. "I was just wondering where you put my suitcases."

"No, Kian, just wait, please," Rhys pleaded. "I'm coming home. Don't go anywhere till I get there."

"I wasn't just going to disappear, Rhys. I just need to

get everything packed. I was going to say goodbye, I promise."

"But you can't leave—you just can't, Kee." Rhys sounded upset, and my stomach rolled.

"I'm coming home. Just wait," Rhys said. "Promise."

"Well, you hid my luggage." I reminded him and even managed a small smile.

"I'm coming home," Rhys said. "I'm on my way." I heard an engine come on.

I took the rest of the clothes off the hanger and folded everything so I was ready when he showed up. I walked to the ensuite and grabbed all my things too. My heart felt like it was being put through the grinder.

I sighed and turned to leave, but I felt faint and had to grab hold of the sink to keep from falling. I drew in a breath and let it out slowly, again and again until I didn't feel like I would puke.

Maybe I needed to eat; I hadn't really had an appetite the last few days—I guess it was finally catching up with me.

I walked slowly back into my room and lowered myself to the bed. But that queasy feeling didn't leave. I leaned back so I was flat in bed, and that was where Rhys found me.

"You're still here," he sighed, relief in his voice.

I chuckled and sat up slowly. "Well, my only other choice was putting all my clothes and shoes in the backseat and trunk of my car."

Rhys shrugged, then took a seat beside me. "I don't want you to go."

"I have to." I sighed, leaning my head on his shoulder.

"No, you don't. Even if you and Gabe can't figure your stuff out, I'm here," Rhys whispered.

"I know, and you'll always be my best friend." I nudged him.

"But you're set on leaving," Rhys sighed. "It's already late today, so maybe wait one more day?" He sighed. "I really don't want you to leave, Kee."

"I know."

14

GABE

AFTER GETTING AN ASS-KICKING FROM MY BROTHER Hunter, who thought I was an idiot for having a chance with a mate that wanted me and fucking it up, I was finally here.

I parked outside the Kincaids' house. They lived in one of the older estates in town, not that you could tell because every house on Longcreek Drive was very well maintained. I parked in the driveway and drew in a breath. Truth was, I didn't even know what I was looking for here.

But maybe seeing a couple like Kian and me would help. Although calling us a couple was stretching it. *And whose fault is that?*

I'd done a lot of berating since Friday, and it hadn't done me any good, so I opened the door and got out. I walked to the front door but couldn't seem to bring myself to ring the bell.

What if… *Oh, shut it*, I told my brain. I'd also what-
ifed enough. I pushed the doorbell, and the door was
pulled open immediately, like someone had been
waiting on the other side. That was how preoccupied I
was. I hadn't even heard.

"Gabe, I was surprised to get your call," Mark said.

I smiled at the burly, bearded alpha. "Thanks for
seeing me on such short notice."

"Of course, come on in." He stepped aside and
opened the door further for me.

I walked into the house, and he shut the door before
leading us into a living room. My eyes immediately
landed on the large family photo that took pride of
place above the sideboard. It had Mark and his omega,
I assumed, Thomas. He was a handsome man that
reminded me of that actor from *Station 19*, the one
married to Bailey from *Grey's Anatomy*. I knew that
because Bailey, my assistant, loved her and chatted
about the show a lot. I'd even watched episodes when I
was over visiting. There were three kids in the picture,
two teenagers and one that was maybe ten or so. They
were a beautiful family.

I turned and found the other alpha watching me.

"You have a beautiful family," I said.

He beamed and looked over at the picture, "I do.
I've been blessed." He gestured to one of the sofas.
"Please take a seat." I nodded and lowered myself to the
sofa nearest to me while he took a seat on the one
across from it. "So," he prompted, "you were quite

vague on the phone. You said there was something you wanted to ask me. We've just finished tax season, so I know it's not about that."

"No, it's not," I agreed. I cleared my throat. "I guess I wanted to ask you about your mate." Mark sat up, and the friendly look left his face.

"What about my mate?" he asked. From the growly timbre of his voice, I could tell his bear was close to the surface.

"I meant your mating," I quickly corrected. I might have been in charge of the den, but I knew not to piss off a bear about his mate or family. My words didn't seem to help, and the scowl on his face deepened, and his eyes narrowed. "What about it?" he demanded.

"I'm fucking this up." I sighed, raking my fingers through my hair.

"How about you start from the beginning," Mark suggested, his tone not quite as angry but still tense.

I met his gaze. "I met my mate," I said, "and he's human."

"Ahh." What was left of the anger drained away, and his eyes filled with understanding. "Let me guess, he doesn't know what we are, and you don't know how or if you should tell him?"

"Ding ding ding, got it in one."

He belly-laughed at my response, all the while nodding. "I get it—trust me, I do. Seventeen years ago, I probably had every thought now running through your head. I was at college when I scented him, and he was so handsome and perfect…and my bear was screaming at me to just go and claim him." He snorted. "What does the beast know?"

We shared an understanding look, and for the first time since I'd laid eyes on Kian, I felt like someone had found the remote and was finally turning down the noise in my head.

"I wondered if I could stay in the city and never shift again and just have a normal life with my mate," he admitted. "Not so easy a choice for you, now is it?" Just having someone speak thoughts I'd had out loud made me feel a little less off-balance. Gods, that was a feeling I wasn't accustomed to and damn sure didn't appreciate.

"I did something stupid," Mark admitted.

I raised a brow and barely stopped myself from saying *spit it out*. But he must have read it on my face because he chuckled but carried on speaking.

"I asked him out on a date, spent every moment with him, fell completely and irrevocably in love…"

"Uh, I'm not sure I understand," I said.

"Well, it might have been easier to leave him alone to go have a normal life if I didn't know how amazing he was," Mark said.

I snorted. That was such horsecrap.

"Okay, no, it wouldn't." Mark stroked his beard, a small smile on his face. "From the moment I scented him, I knew I would give up everything to make him mine."

"Yeah," was all I could manage.

"The crazy thing is he could tell something was eating me up inside." Mark's tone was musing. "I felt like there was this huge part of myself I couldn't share with him, and I wanted to share everything with him."

Exactly. That was it.

"The truth is I had to trust that the Gods knew what they were doing, trust that I knew my mate, even though we'd been together like a month."

"How did you do that?" I asked.

Mark leaned forward. "Well, I realized that I had to take a leap of faith. The truth was I could have told him and shown him, and he could have run in the other direction." He blew out a breath. "I had that nightmare on repeat for a few nights."

"Same here," I admitted.

"Then there's the possibility he'd go off and tell the wrong person," Mark added. "I was terrified of putting my parents, siblings, grandparents in danger." Mark gave me a speculative look. "I bet for you, you've added the whole town to that equation."

I hung my head. "So what did you do?" I had to remind myself this story had a happy ending. The proof was on the wall.

"It came down to telling him the truth and having a life with him or losing him," Mark said.

"But you could have never told him," I pointed out. "Lived somewhere else and only shifted maybe when you came here and had time to yourself."

Mark inclined his head. "I could have, but we both know that our bears are a huge part of who we are. Not only that, but they're possessive assholes. They'd want to meet their mate too."

That was true. I wanted my mate to know my bear; he was me as much as I was him.

"I also convinced myself if he went and reported me, they would throw him in a psychiatric ward," Mark said dryly.

"Well, isn't that a cheery thought." I groaned and sighed.

"You know what I think?" Mark asked but didn't wait for a reply. "I think we focus on the fact that it would be easier if they were a shifter because they'd know what we are, but the fact is—and you can ask your parents—you still have to make it work with your mate. Compromise, get to know them. All being a shifter does is give both of you a bit of certainty that this person is yours. But the fact is we have something that I see as a gift." He paused and held my gaze. Clearly, he wanted me to ask. So I did.

"What's that?"

"He chose you," Mark said simply. "There's no animal guiding him. Maybe there's a little helping hand from the Gods because I do believe the mate bond starts to form regardless of whether or not your mate is a human or a shifter. But they're choosing you without the certainty. Wanting you without the certainty. There's something quite wonderful about it," Mark said.

I let his words wash over me, and it hit me for the truth that it was. My mate had chosen me. Even with me being an ass, he'd wanted me. And he deserved my trust and a huge apology for being an idiot.

A door opened, and footsteps pounded down the stairs, and a curly-haired child ran into the room before stopping short at seeing me. "Daddy?"

Mark opened his arms and got an armful of kid. "Say hello to Gabe," he whispered to the kid who'd buried their face in his chest.

They peeked out, and I got a shy smile. "Hello, Gabe."

Mark beamed at the child in his arms before looking up at me, "This is Riley. She ate too many sweets with her brothers, forgetting they're twice her size, and ended up home with a tummy ache." He tickled her, and she giggled.

Then and there, I saw my future. And I wanted it. I wanted to leap and trust the amazing man the Gods had seen fit to give me.

Like he could read my thoughts, Mark said, "My leap paid off."

I jumped on my feet. "I gotta go," I said, heading for the door, not even waiting for Mark to see me out. "Thank you," I called, striding out of the house and breaking into a jog down the driveway to get to my car.

I didn't go through town on my way home, so I

could drive as fast as I could to get to my mate. I didn't want to wait one more minute to tell him everything and apologize for being so horrible to him. I knew I would spend the rest of my life making it up to him if he would have me…all of me.

I wanted to call, but of course my battery was dead. I'd barely remembered to charge it the last couple of days. Hell, I didn't have a charger till Bailey came over yesterday and threw it at me, literally.

It took less than ten minutes to get back on the ranch, although I came in through one of the back entrances, not the front gate. Which meant it took a little longer to get to the house when I was actually back on our land. I didn't even bother stopping at my house. I pulled up in front of Rhys's and jumped out of the car without even turning it off.

I was at the front door and pushing on the doorbell while also banging on the door, but I stopped because I knew deep down my mate wasn't there. I could feel him when he was close, and he wasn't.

The door opened, but I was already almost at my car, but I turned to find my younger brother and my papa. "Kian! Where is he? Is he at the office? I need to talk to him."

I was back to my car when my brother's words hit me like a Mack truck. "He left."

I spun around. "What?" I whispered.

"He just left," Papa said. "I tried to keep him here, but…he left."

My brother was just shooting me daggers, but I ignored him. "What? Where? When?" I bent over, trying to catch my breath from what felt like a sucker punch. "Where is he? Please tell me you know where he is."

Rhys sighed and came up beside me. "You better not fuck this up," he snapped.

"I won't. I promise." I couldn't even get mad at my brother for the rebuke because I had fucked up.

"He just left"—Rhys pulled his phone out—"like five minutes ago. Papa and I stalled as long as we could, hoping you weren't a total idiot." As Rhys spoke, he pulled his phone out. He tapped for a second, then met my gaze. "He's not gotten to the front gate yet. He said he wanted to stop and drop a gift off for Bailey."

Before he finished his sentence, I shifted and took off. The last thing I heard was my brother saying he would follow in the car.

It would have been a little faster in the car, but I knew a shortcut that would bring me out on the road. I pushed my bear as much as I could and came out a couple of miles before the gate and parked myself in the middle of the road.

I heard a car coming and hoped it was my mate and I hadn't in fact missed him. When I saw it was his car, I stood on my hind legs to make sure he saw me.

I saw his eyes widen—I knew he was far enough to brake in time, so I waited till he came to a complete stop. His eyes were on me, and he had both arms on the wheel. It took me by surprise when the door opened and Kian stepped out.

Right then and there, I knew my mate would accept me. And maybe Mark was right—maybe there was a part of our mates that knew us even in this form. Because sane people would run and scream or at least back away. I made a mental note to make sure he knew not all wild animals were shifters, and sometimes flight was a good way to go.

As my mate approached me, his eyes wide and mouth open, I drew in a breath, wanting to fill my senses with that scent I'd missed as I waited where I was for him.

My eyes widened, and I took in another whiff to make sure I wasn't wrong. By the time he was standing in front of me, I knew without a doubt: my mate was pregnant.

15

KIAN

I SHOULD HAVE BEEN TERRIFIED OF THE BEAR ON ITS HIND legs that could probably crush my windshield if it wanted to, but for some reason, I wasn't. There was something familiar about it. I could swear it was the same one from that night.

A car pulled up behind me, and I turned to see who it was. Rhys was in Gabe's car, but he didn't move to get out. It sounded ridiculous, but to me, that told me he thought it was safe. I knew my best friend, and he would have done everything he could to protect me if he thought I was in danger. Even if that meant running headfirst towards it.

With somewhat of a blessing from Rhys, I turned back to the bear, who seemed to have stayed completely still the whole time, but had its eyes firmly on me. I should have felt like prey as I got closer to this apex predator, but just like the last time—maybe even more so—I didn't feel like I was in danger. It almost felt like it was waiting for me to approach.

And not in the *I want to bathe in your entrails so come closer* kind of way.

When there was barely any space between us, there was a movement, and right before my eyes, the bear changed. Fur disappeared and the face changed, until the one man that I'd been dying to come after me was in front of me. And suddenly, everything clicked into place.

I opened my mouth, but the only thing that came out was, "You're naked." For some reason, laughter erupted from my mouth. "You're naked."

Gabe's brows turned down, and I took another step towards him. We weren't quite touching, but it was close. He held my gaze as he said, "A man could get a complex when laughter is the only reaction he gets standing naked in front of his person."

My brain stalled on 'his person.' Was that how Gabe saw me? I hadn't been wrong believing there was something between us. I hadn't been wrong thinking he felt it too. The voice that had said it was too soon tried to chime in, but I put it on mute.

I gave him a once-over, my eyes traveling down his body. I couldn't help it—I was only human, and Gabe was stunning. From the top of his rich, chocolate-brown hair to the muscled column of his throat, down to his perfectly sculpted biceps. I was pretty sure drool escaped at the sight of the V. Was there anything hotter? I wanted to trace him with my tongue. His thick cock that had filled me so good. His muscled thighs with a fine dusting of hair. The man was a walking wet dream. I could still remember his arms holding me up against the wall as he'd thrust into me.

Focus, Kian.

"Trust me, that's not why I'm laughing. You're perfect." I reached out to touch him but dropped my hands before I did.

Gabe took my hand and placed it on his chest. "You can always touch me, Kian. Always."

I met his gaze and looked away quickly. "I was just thinking about the day Rhys told me to pass you the honey after I'd brought it out for the bear...for you, I guess. I knew there was something familiar about it, which is crazy because, you know, it was a bear..." I pulled my hand from over his heart where he'd put it. "But I suppose it was also you."

Gabe's lips lifted slightly, but then he sighed and put his finger under my chin and lifted it so we were looking at each other. "I'm so sorry, Kian. For everything." He hung his head, and his shoulders slumped. He looked absolutely dejected. The guilt and remorse poured off him in waves.

I thought about it logically, and there was no doubt I hated the way things had gone after our first time together, but with this new information, I kind of got it. This was a huge secret. A life-changing, world-altering secret, and Gabe couldn't just blurt it out in a conversation. I would bet there were rules about even telling. I would imagine they went to extreme lengths to guard this truth for fear of being exploited, feared, and hunted. If Rhys could, he would have told me because Rhys told me everything. So I knew he hadn't been able to share this.

But Gabe had broken the rules for me. He didn't have to tell me; he could have simply let me leave. But he showed himself, put everything on the line just to make me stay.

At least, I hoped that was why. I really did.

I slipped my hand into his and squeezed. "Can we talk in the car? You're kind of naked in the middle of the road, for everyone to see." I really didn't want anyone else seeing Gabe like this. He was mine. A deep, very instinctive part of me knew it.

Fuck! I had never felt like this before. So possessive of another human being. It was both thrilling and scary because that just meant the heartbreak could wreck me.

"I kind of love that you care about my modesty." Gabe's voice was teasing. "Come on." He led me to the car and put me in the passenger side before going over to the driver's. I saw him wave, and I realized I'd completely forgotten about Rhys.

Suddenly, all those moments when it'd felt like Rhys had wanted to tell me something but stopped himself made sense. I would speak to my best friend, and we would be fine. I knew it, but right now, I needed Gabe.

I squeezed my eyes shut at the thought. Yeah, it was definitely scary, especially after Friday, but could I really hold it against him? What was it like having such a monumental secret?

Gabe sat sideways with his legs hanging out of the car as he moved the seat all the way back. I smiled because I really did love how much bigger he was than me.

When Gabe finally got in the car, he twisted his body so he was facing me. He was still shirtless, and I couldn't help it. I traced his chest, but of course I couldn't stop there. My eyes wandered lower, and I was a little disappointed to see he'd found some sweats.

Probably, Rhys had brought a pair for him.

Rhys. I looked in the mirror and found he'd left. I'd forgotten about my best friend completely. Way to go, Kian.

Who could blame him, though? Seeing Gabe naked reminded me of how much pleasure his body had brought mine. My chest tightened at what had followed, though—the aftermath.

I drew in a long breath, then let it out slowly before screwing up the courage to ask, "Was this... This was the only reason why you..." Even while my heart said that was why—it had to be—I couldn't seem to complete the sentence. I wrapped my arms around myself and closed my eyes, trying not to relive the moment.

Gabe lifted me out of my seat, and I eeped as I was

placed in his lap. His arms tightened around me, and he buried his face in my neck.

We sat like that for… I wasn't sure how long until he cupped my cheek. I leaned back so I could see him, and I read guilt in on his face.

"I am so sorry for hurting you, Kian." Gabe's usually deep voice was wobbly. "Gods. I fucked up. I am so sorry." He put his head on my chest. "I didn't want to lie to you, but I didn't know… There's no excuse." Gabe sighed. "Please forgive me, Kian."

Hearing how broken up he was about it, knowing it wasn't something I did, soothed my jagged heart and started knitting it back together.

"I want to tell you everything," Gabe whispered.

I chuckled and ran my hands through his hair. Gabe groaned his pleasure, and I grinned.

"I have so many questions." I leaned into his chest and sighed. "But maybe we can move out of the middle of the road to have this conversation."

Gabe smiled against my neck. "I kind of like the feel of you in my arms."

I shivered at his warm breath against my skin and shifted in his lap. Gabe moaned and nipped my earlobe, making me squirm even more.

"Kian." Gabe growled my name, and I pressed my forehead to his. "Gabe."

His hands wrapped around my waist. "Gabe," I sighed.

I brushed my lips over his. It was the lightest of

kisses, but I felt it through my whole body. Gabe's arms tightened around me.

His lips were so close, and I couldn't help it, I leaned in for another kiss. I needed to taste him again.

Gabe let me control the kiss until I pulled back. The smile on his face was soft.

I stroked his jaw and across his lips, and his eyes darkened. They were as dark as they'd been when he was a bear, and he growled. My breath caught.

There was that look again, like I was spinning out into oblivion. Gabe made me feel more than I'd ever thought I could, but it was everything I'd ever wanted.

It was a look I recognized from my parents, even Jonathan and Stefan, and as much as I'd wanted it, I never thought I'd get it.

Gabe growled, "If we don't stop this now…" He sighed. "As much as I want to keep going, I don't want to rush you. I need you to know this isn't just sex for me."

Maybe it was reckless, but I believed him.

"I know." I exhaled and repeated, "I know."

He held my gaze, and I saw the desperate hope there. "Please forgive me, Kian." His voice was a whispered growl.

"I do," I whispered, curling into his body even deeper, as uncomfortable as it was in the car.

We sat there for a little while until I yawned. Gabe nudged me slightly. "Come on, let's go home."

I yawned again and nodded. "I don't know why I'm so tired."

Gabe helped me back into my seat and took my hand. "Let's get you home. We have a lot to talk about."

I STRETCHED but didn't open my eyes. Huh, how had I gotten in bed? Then everything flooded back, and my stomach dropped. For a second, I worried it had all been a dream.

The door opened, and my stomach dropped. What if I woke up back in Rhys's guest room?

"I know you're awake." At the sound of that voice, I finally let out the breath I'd been holding. The bed dipped next to me.

I opened my eyes slowly and came face to face with Gabe, and I couldn't help it. My lips curved in a huge smile.

"So it wasn't a dream," I murmured.

Gabe shook his head, but I read worry on his face. "Still okay with everything?"

It clicked. Gabe was worried I'd slept on it and thought I would freak out or something.

"You mean the whole 'you changing into a bear' thing?" I teased.

"Yeah, that." His brow smoothed, and a small smile appeared on his face.

"I think Rhys is still Rhys. I just know one more

thing about him. And you're still the man that I want to get to know better."

Gabe beamed, and the smile hit me in the feels. My words had made him happy, and a little more of that fear from how the other night had gone dissipated.

"I want to know everything about you too, Kian," Gabe said. "And that means you can ask me anything."

I thought about it, and as fantastical as it was, I didn't have any pressing questions. "Oh, does it hurt when you shift?"

Gabe shook his head. "Not even a little. My bear is a part of me, and the transition is usually seamless."

"He's really big," I said. "Like huge. But I guess that makes sense 'cause you are too." I tried not to think about naked Gabe, but it was hard.

Gabe's eyes danced almost like he could read my thoughts. God, I hoped not.

"I know I said this already," Gabe started. He looked away and began rubbing the back of his neck. "But I need to apologize again."

I put my hand on his thigh. "You really don't have to —" I interrupted.

"No, please let me." Gabe covered my hand on his thigh. "I really tried," he sighed. "I kind of let my bear take over, or maybe that's the excuse I used... I wanted you, still do, but I needed you to know everything—" He took a sharp breath. "After I felt like I'd lied to you..." His voice trailed off, and he raked his hand through his hair.

"It hurt," I admitted. "And I never want to feel like that again."

"I swear on my life, Kian, I will never do anything to hurt you again, not intentionally." Gabe held my gaze like he needed me to see he was being honest.

I believed him. It was crazy and maybe stupid of me. But I believed him. Now that I knew and I was certain I hadn't manufactured the attraction between us in my head. "I believe you." I slipped my hand from under his and cupped his cheek. "I really do, and at least of all the reasons I thought, I never figured hey, he turns into a bear… It's a pretty good one."

Gabe snorted.

"Well, if that was the only reason our date got ruined." I bit my lip, hoping I wasn't being too forward. "I was thinking maybe we could do a do-over?"

Gabe's eyes lit up. "I would love that." His high cheekbones flushed red. "I made lunch while you were asleep. I was restless, and my bear wanted to take care of you."

My heart flipped, and I threw myself in his arms and kissed him. Gabe's arm went around my waist, and his tongue licked into me, and I felt his hard cock against my thigh. I squirmed, and Gabe moaned and deepened the kiss. I slipped my hands into his hair and moaned, but then Gabe pulled back and placed his head on my shoulder. Gabe groaned. "I really want to do this, but there's something I should tell you first."

My heart skipped a beat, but it hit me. I either trusted Gabe or didn't…

"I hear your heart racing," Gabe whispered. "But I swore I'd never hurt you, Kian, and I know I have to earn that trust."

I shook my head. "No. No. I trust you. I do."

"It's nothing bad. I swear. At least, I hope you don't think it is. I think it's a good thing, the best thing to ever happen to me, really…"

I'd never heard him sound so unsure of himself.

I turned so I was straddling his thighs and looking him in the eye. I took his face in my hands. "I know this is crazy for me to say, but something inside of me is saying this is something special." I nibbled on my lips, trying to decide if this was too forward. But what the heck? "I've never felt like this about anyone before, and maybe it's absolutely crazy, but I think maybe this could be something serious," I blurted out in one breath before I lost my nerve.

Gabe grinned and stole my lips in a searing kiss, then pulled back. "You have no idea how happy it makes me to hear you say that."

"Good." I grinned and squirmed in his lap again. "About picking up where we left off…"

Gabe chuckled and gripped my hips, holding me in place, which didn't help since I could feel his still very hard, oooh-so-thick cock. If we were naked, it would be teasing my hole. I shivered at the memory of that sweet, perfect stretch followed by the fullness that was almost too much but was just perfect.

He moaned and nipped my neck. "Hold that thought," he whispered.

I chuckled and ground my hips. I loved how Gabe reacted to me. It was a heady feeling.

Gabe leaned back so he could look at me. There was worry in his eyes still, but not as bad as before. "You're my mate." The way he said *mate* was almost reverent, and it stirred something deep inside of me.

"Mate?" I felt like I knew what that meant, but I think I needed him to say it.

Gabe bobbed his head. "Mate," he repeated. "I guess the easiest way to describe it would be soulmate...but it's more than that. For a shifter, you get one, one person that completes you. One person that you wait for and hope that you find to spend your life with."

That was what I'd thought he meant. "And that's me?" My heart was racing. "Me?"

"Yes, you, Kian." Gabe's hands rubbed up and down my back. "You're everything to me, everything I've been waiting for." He tucked his head in my neck and breathed in deeply. "Mine," he growled.

The word, the way he said it, had goose pimples appearing all over my skin, and I shivered. It sounded so right.

Gabe bit down on my neck, and my dick leaked. "I want to mark you, Kian, claim you as mine. Please say yes." His voice was so deep and gravelly; it felt like it was ripped from his soul. "From the moment I saw you, I wanted you. I wanted to know everything about you. Touch you, taste you, mark you so there'd be no doubt that you're mine."

I groaned and nodded. "Yes." I was following my instinct, and I trusted it and Gabe. "Claim me." His eyes didn't waver. His voice was steady and firm. Everything I was, everything in me, said to believe him. So I was taking the leap because I was head over heels for this man.

Gabe stroked my lips with his thumb. "I will never want anyone else, never desire anyone else. Mates can't be unfaithful once they're claimed. That's just how things work in our world. You know what that means, Kian. You'll be mine, forever."

The words were like a vow. One that I'd been searching for since I understood what it meant to be loved and cherished, seeing my parents' relationship. I felt the rightness in every part of me. Besides, if it was a dream, it was a dream come true. "Forever sounds perfect to me."

At my words, he slammed our mouths together, his arms binding around me. My world turned on its axis, and I groaned as he buried his fingers in my hair, holding me close as he ravaged my mouth. My heart raced with excitement as I gave myself freely to the passion of this moment and this man…what it meant.

I groaned and opened my mouth, allowing Gabe in.

He moved his tongue against mine, touching, caressing. Every touch felt like heaven, but I wanted more.

I almost protested when Gabe pulled away, but then small kisses were pressed against the skin of my throat.

When Gabe pulled my shirt up, I sat up and lifted my arms. He tossed it aside, and his mouth latched onto my nipple.

"Ooooh," I moaned as pleasure flooded my body.

Gabe stood, his arms around my waist, supporting me. Then, gently, he lay me down on the bed.

He took his shirt off, and I licked my lips. He would never stop being gorgeous to me. If I'd sculpted my perfect man, I don't think I would have done as good a job.

He knelt on the bed, straddling me, then leaned in for another kiss. My hands stroked every inch of that glorious exposed skin I could get to. I loved how big and strong Gabe was. It made me feel safe and protected. And it was really hot.

"I've wanted you in my bed for so long," he sighed. "Your scent on my sheets." He growled, stealing another kiss before kissing his way down my neck back to my chest.

"Your body is amazing, perfect for me," Gabe said before he took my nipple in his warm mouth. I sucked in a breath.

"That feels good. So good," I moaned.

He gave the other one the same attention, and my cock leaked, but all I could do was whimper. Gabe kissed down my belly before moving to unzip my shorts.

He pulled them off, and I lifted for him, pushing my briefs down too.

Gabe sat back and seemed to be taking in my body. "You're stunning, Kian." I'd never heard such reverence in anyone's voice about me before. It was both hot and humbling.

He stood up and pushed down the sweatpants he was wearing, and I watched him, completely enthralled. He settled between my legs and licked the precum leaking from my tip like it was a popsicle on a hot summer day. I moaned and slipped my hands through his hair. Gabe took my whole cock deep into his mouth, sucking it in.

"Oh. Oh. Fuck," I cried. My hands tightened in his hair, and I bucked my hips as pleasure engulfed me.

The suction around my dick grew stronger, tighter. I could feel the pressure building. I was so close, fuck.

His mouth swirled and sucked its way back up to the head of my cock, where he licked and kissed the tip again. Gabe sucked my cock up, down and around, making me feel melty, blissful. I inhaled sharply when I felt a finger inside my slick hole. I groaned and cried out.

Gabe twisted his finger around until he hit that sweet spot inside me. "Fuck." My body arched into the air, and an orgasm of epic proportions raced through me, stealing my breath.

Gabe moved up the bed and lifted me so I was on his lap as I tried to catch my breath. I sighed and tucked my face in his neck and breathed in. I loved his musky, earthy smell. Like sandalwood, lemon, and something smoky.

He stroked down my back, holding me close, but I was already recovering from my first orgasm, and I was ready for more. I licked up his neck and loved how his big body went still.

It was heady knowing how I affected him. I trailed my hand down his chest, tracing his muscles. My mate —gosh, that sounded great—stayed still and let me explore. I used my nail to tease the tight buds of his nipples. And his body jerked. I looked up at him and found his intense gaze on me. "You're beautiful," I sighed.

Gabe's eyes softened, but before he could speak, I covered his sensitive nipple with my mouth and was rewarded with a moan. I moved so I straddled his thigh, and I watched Gabe watching me, but he never spoke.

I leaned forward and kissed him, and his hand moved into my hair as our tongues tangled. When I finally broke away, we were both breathing heavily.

Finally, I traced the dusting of hair down to the perfect gift they led to. Gabe's breath hitched when I teased the thick head of his cock, over the slit. I lifted a pearl of precum on my finger and met his gaze as I licked it.

Gabe's eyes darkened completely, and I realized he had the dark eyes of his bear at that moment. His stomach muscles tightened, and his hands bunched the sheets. I teased the sensitive head of his cock, focusing on the slit with my pinkie.

When it looked like he was about to snap and grab me, I wrapped my hand around his thick cock and lowered my mouth to his cock, wrapping my tongue around the head and sucking. The sound Gabe made was damn near animalistic, and his hand landed on my head.

I used my tongue to trace up and down his hard cock, learning every vein, every ridge. I teased the slit with my tongue while stroking him and listening as each touch drove him higher and higher. Slick flooded my channel as I sucked him. God, I couldn't wait to have him inside me again.

I wrapped my hands around the base of his cock and sucked Gabe down. Fuck, he was thick and long. My eyes watered as the thick head brushed against the back of my throat, but I didn't stop. I pulled off and took more of him until I had most of his cock in my mouth. Gabe cursed, and his hand tightened in my hair.

I began to work his cock over and over again, taking it deep into my throat each time and swallowing around the thick head. Gabe finally pulled me off him. "I'm going to come," he ground out, "and this time, baby, I want it to be inside you."

His words thrummed through my body, and my hole clenched. "Yes," I sighed. I wanted that—boy, did I want that.

Gabe lifted me off him and flipped our positions. He knelt on the bed, and I followed him with my eyes. He was so sexy, and it hit me that he was all mine. Of all the people in the world, fate or whatever it was—I made a mental note to ask—had chosen Gabe for me.

Me. It was like the prayers I'd said standing alone at the cemetery had all been answered. A man I could build a life and a family with. I got that in one swoop with Gabe's parents and siblings. Someone who would notice if I didn't come home at night. My very own alpha who would hold me at night and remind me I wasn't alone.

Gabe looked at me like he wanted to ravage. His eyes were hungry, and as he covered my body with his, it was easy to see the apex predator right now because I felt like prey. Very enthusiastic prey, though.

Even though I could see how turned on he was, Gabe's touch was gentle. His hands traced down my skin, and my body thrummed with anticipation.

I loved how his body covered mine like he was protecting me from the rest of the world. Gabe sealed his lips to mine, and all I could do was respond. He deepened the kiss even as I felt his finger rub against my hole. I moaned and arched, my hole begging to be filled.

Gabe broke our kiss and whispered, "I want the taste of your slick on my tongue."

My body trembled at what he meant. "Oh God." I'd never done that before.

"I'll take that as a yes," he murmured. Gabe moved so fast it barely registered. The next thing I knew, my knees were pushed apart, and his hot, wet mouth was on my crease. His tongue trailed from my ass to my balls and then pressed inside before pulling back again. He teased into my hole with the tip of his tongue, and my brain short-circuited. His beard stubble against my tender skin drove me higher as he sucked and fucked his way inside my body with his tongue.

"So sweet," Gabe moaned. "All mine."

"Oh God," I moaned. I'd never felt soo—"Nggnhh."

I felt those thick digits slide inside me, stretching and opening me up, and all I could do was whimper and beg.

My skin felt too tight, and I was so close again. I couldn't take it—I needed more. His tip nudged my entrance, and I closed my eyes in anticipation of that first stretch.

Gabe stole my lips in a kiss as he pushed into my body. God, that stretch and burn as he entered me was as good as I remembered.

I drew in a deep breath and tried to relax through it, and Gabe went slow, giving me time to adjust. Even though I was so slick, he was so big.

Gabe's forehead was creased in concentration as he

moved slowly until he was all the way in. God, I loved the feeling of being stretched around him. I let out a big sigh and groaned in pleasure.

"Please," I begged.

That seemed to be what Gabe was waiting for. He began thrusting in and out, starting off slowly as I moaned through every move he made. Fuck, it felt so damn good to be filled up again. To feel the stretch and fullness of his cock inside me. His big, strong body weighing me down as he thrust into me.

The man above me looked at me like I was a rare piece of art he couldn't believe he'd come across.

I lifted my ass, meeting every thrust and growl, and he began to pound me harder. I wanted to feel him for days. I never wanted to wonder again if this was a dream.

Gabe's thrusts became frantic, and he crushed his lips to mine, devouring my mouth. He broke our kiss and flipped me over like I weighed nothing, I went on my hands and knees, ass in the air, and Gabe grabbed my hips in what would surely be a bruising grip and slammed back in. It was almost too much, but not enough at the same time.

"Please," I cried. He began to pound into me, his hands on my hip tightening. And I knew I would surely wear his mark.

Gabe lifted me off my hands so his sweat-slicked body was pressed against my back. He hit my prostate on every thrust. "Gabe, please..." I whimpered as I felt my orgasm cresting.

"Come for me, mate," he growled into my ear.

Like it was ripped from his words, my climax hit, streams of come jetting out as I cried out and convulsed around him. My body squeezed Gabe's, and I heard him gasp and curse.

"Tell me you're mine, Kian," Gabe demanded in a rough tone that told me he was close to his own release.

"Yes," I cried out. "I'm yours. Yours, Gabe."

His cock pulsed at my declaration. "Mine!" Gabe snarled in return as he nuzzled my neck, licking and nipping. A low rumble sounded in his throat as he sank his teeth into the soft skin between my neck and collarbone.

As he bit down, Gabe came deep inside me. Pain hit me, but on its heels came lip biting, toe curling pleasure. It was like the Fourth of July behind my eyes. I felt Gabe's cock, already hard and huge in my ass, thicken more, if that was possible, as he filled my channel with his cum.

Gabe held me tightly to him as he shouted my name. I gasped when the stretch got even more intense. Our bodies shook, our skin was slick with sweat, and our hearts pounded. After several beats of nothing but the sound of our breathing, they slowed down.

"Oh wow." Gabe's voice held earnest surprise.

"What? What?" I asked even as shocks of pleasure seemed to be going through me still.

"I just got my knot for the first time." Gabe sounded utterly pleased with himself.

"What's that?" I asked, brow furrowing.

"When a shifter meets and claims his mate, a knot forms at the base of his cock, keeping him locked inside of his mate." I didn't miss the wonder in Gabe's voice.

"It didn't happen last time," I pointed out. Gabe lay us down gently so we were on our sides. "Why now?"

"Because I claimed you." There was that pride-filled tone again.

I chuckled. "Ahh."

Gabe was mine. And I guess if I'd had any doubts, there was a physical sign.

Gabe's arms tightened around me, and he leaned up on his elbow and examined the bite wound he'd left, tracing it gently. Then I felt his lips brush over it.

"Will it scar?" I asked.

"Yes. But only lightly. It will let shifters know we're mated." Again, there was deep satisfaction in his voice.

I grinned at the pride he felt for claiming me. "You're happy about that," I said.

"Happier than I've ever been, baby," Gabe said and kissed the mark again.

"You're mine now."

I grinned. "I'm good with that."

I'd never felt so content before, and I dozed off a

little, secure that this time I would be waking up in Gabe's arms.

I wasn't sure how much time had passed when I finally felt the knot recede. My life was so weird. *Not that you're complaining.*

Gabe groaned as his softening cock slid slowly from my body. And I missed the fullness.

Still, I couldn't stop smiling as Gabe nuzzled the mate mark on my neck. He tenderly stroked my sweat-damp hair.

"So." I turned so I was facing Gabe. The happy and contented look on his face made my heart sing. "Do I get a knot every time?" I asked.

Gabe chuckled. "Like it, do you?" he teased.

I shrugged. "Wasn't bad."

Gabe snorted and tickled me. "I'll show you 'wasn't bad.'"

We ended up kissing again until we both had to break apart for air.

"I have so much to learn," I said.

"I'll help, my love, and so will Rhys and my papa, trust me. You're family now."

Family. That sounded perfect.

I really wished my parents could have gotten to meet Gabe. My papa had always said *find someone that deserves you*. I had a feeling Papa would agree that Gabe did.

16

GABE

I COULDN'T REMEMBER EVER BEING SO HAPPY. MY BEAR was purring in happiness even though the beast still wanted to be officially introduced to our mate. But there was time enough for that. Kian was here. He was mine. And he was claimed.

I hummed as I plated the fresh bread that Graham had dropped off for me. I looked at the tray: sausage, eggs, bread, waffles... "Ooh, syrup." I headed to the fridge and grabbed it and put it on the plate. I spun around. "Juice. Or should I get water...maybe both. Definitely both."

I grabbed everything and cursed when I heard the movement upstairs. I'd been planning to be there when Kian woke up. But my bear also wanted to feed him, and of course, I could have run out and grabbed some-thing, but I wanted to cook it for him with my hands in our home. My bear was riding me, especially with our mate pregnant.

Which is something you still need to tell him. And I would. I promised never to lie to him, so no more waiting. I'd gotten sidetracked last night…a lot. I couldn't help smiling, thinking about how acquainted with his body I'd gotten last night.

I heard the toilet flush and grabbed my tray and got moving. I hurried up the stairs and opened the door to the bedroom just as Kian came out of the bathroom.

"I come bearing breakfast." I held the tray up and walked it over to the sitting area in my room, then paused. "Actually bed or sofa?" I asked.

Kian came up to me and wrapped his arms around my waist from behind and leaned his head on my back. "You made breakfast?"

"Well, I had to feed my mate. We did burn quite a few calories last night."

"And this morning," Kian helpfully added.

"And this morning," I agreed, smiling. "So breakfast," I said.

Kian came around front and went on his tiptoes. I happily obliged, kissing him sweetly. We finally pulled back, and I said, "Go on, sit down. Let me feed my mate."

He grinned and hurried over to the sofa and sat with his leg folded under him. I loved the fact that he'd grabbed my T-shirt from last night and how it hung off him. I really liked him being surrounded by my scent.

I put the tray down on his lap, and before I could straighten, he grabbed my face and planted a kiss on my lips. When he pulled back, he whispered, "This is so sweet. Thank you."

"My pleasure." I grinned. Kian's belly rumbled before I could add anything else. I chuckled and picked up a waffle and held it to his lips. "Open," I instructed.

"You know, that's how some parts of this morning began," he teased.

I leered at him playfully. "Don't tempt me. Now open."

He did as I asked, and I fed the waffle to him. My bear purred in happiness when Kian's eyes lit up. He chewed quickly and grinned. "That's soo good. I didn't know you could cook."

"Well, isn't that part of the whole 'being together' thing...getting to know things about each other?" I pointed out as I took a bite of the waffle. He didn't need to know that this was a just-add-water mix.

Kian beamed. "Most definitely, so what's your favorite color?"

I snorted. "How very first date... Although I don't think anyone ever actually asks that on a first date."

"I can't say I know either way. I've only had three first dates, although I guess two. Does our first time at the café count?" he asked.

"It does to me," I said. "I should have stayed away from you. I'd been trying, but when Rhys called me and said something had happened to your car, I rushed down there so fast. And there you were."

"I thought you didn't like me," Kian admitted. "I remember seeing you the day I pulled up, and you had this weird squinty look in your eyes and a deep frown on your face, and it was like our gazes collided, and you turned and left." Kian lifted another waffle and chewed, then swallowed. "All I could think was crap, maybe moving here hadn't been the best idea."

"Trust me, before I even scented you, I thought you were beautiful." I chuckled, shaking my head. "Then there was a gust of wind that carried your scent right to me." I cupped his face. "I wanted to run to you and pick you up in my arms and never let go. I said a thank you to the Gods for not forgetting about me and sending me my mate. And then I started thinking about how to tell you. How you'd react... Would you run screaming?" I pushed down on my chest, just remembering. "Then I thought maybe it would be okay if you were close by. I could at least see you."

"Wow." Kian's voice was barely above a whisper.

"Then my bear ended up at Rhys's, and there you were. I wasn't paying attention, but I bet my bear scented you and just had to get close. By the time I realized what was happening, I kind of wanted you to meet him. And he wanted you to meet him."

"Even though it took ten years off my life," Kian laughed, "but I don't know. It was weird. I was also drawn to you."

"Well, when you're ready, he wants to meet you officially," I said. All the while holding my breath, waiting to hear what he thought.

Kian beamed at me and kissed me soundly. "I would love to."

My bear hummed his contentment. "Later," I said. "Till then, eat."

Kian did as I asked, but he sighed. "I have to submit a file to a client today, and I have a Skype meeting with a potential new client, and I can't wear your clothes. I've never done the walk of shame. I have to do the walk of shame." Weirdly, he didn't sound upset about it, just amused.

I hoped he wouldn't be upset about what I had to say next. "Well, what if you don't have to?" I rubbed the back of my neck, waiting for his answer.

Kian's brows furrowed. "Have to what?"

"So don't get upset," I said.

His brows went up. "Why would I be upset? Do I have a reason to be upset?"

I picked the tray up, put it on the sofa, and took both his hands in mine, lifting him. Then I led him towards the walk-in and threw the door open.

I leaned against the door and crossed my arms as I watched him. Kian kept turning to look at me as he opened drawers and touched the clothes that had been hung up.

Kian walked back to me and stopped right in front of me. "You did this? You unpacked all my stuff?"

I shrugged. "This is your home, our home, I hope... If it's too much, too soon, I get it. We can get you back at Rhys's." I grimaced at the thought. "I don't want to rush you. Maybe this was too much too soon. I'll help you pack. I assumed. I shouldn't have assumed. I'm so sorry, Kian."

Kian pulled my arms apart and stepped into them. He wrapped his arms around my waist. "Just kiss me."

I cupped his face in both of my hands, "You're not mad?"

Kian shrugged. "Well, I've never moved in with a boyfriend in one day. But deep down, I know it's right, and this"—he gestured to the closet—"it just shows me that you want me. And I guess that's all I need."

"I do, Kian. Always and forever." Boyfriend was too tame a word, but if that was how my mate saw it... It worked for now. Maybe I needed to propose. In his world, that was the equivalent to what we were now. Married.

I leaned forward and took Kian's sweet lips in a kiss. He tasted of waffles and Kian. He was perfection. Our tongues danced to an age-old song. And like every time before, he took my breath away.

I drank him in and wanted more. My hands slid down to his hips and pulled him even closer.

I lifted him off the ground, and his legs wrapped around my waist even as he threaded his hand in my hair and held on. His tongue swirled and explored inside my mouth. Gods, I would never get tired of kissing him.

When we finally pulled back for air, Kian trailed his finger across my lips. "I guess I gotta tell Rhys I'm moving out."

"I believe he already knows, love."

"I guess he does." Kian wiggled to be put down. "I wanna go exploring around the house, but I'm still hungry. You know, I usually do yogurt or something for breakfast." He headed back to the tray.

I blew out a breath. "Well, there's one more thing I have to tell you, actually."

Kian munched on bacon and looked up at me. "What? More life-changing news?"

I closed my eyes and drew in a breath. And I prayed to Urs this wasn't what pushed my mate over the edge.

"I may know why you're a little hungrier than usual." I pushed my hand in my pocket. "I think you're pregnant." I shook my head. "Okay, think isn't the right word. You're pregnant."

Kian laughed. "Ha, ha. Very funny."

I didn't speak.

"You're joking. You can't know that quickly." Kian shook his head. "I know you're a big, strong alpha, but even you can't say for sure," he teased.

I walked over and pushed the coffee table aside so I could kneel in front of him and take his hand in mine. "I'm serious, baby."

Kian studied me, and acceptance seemed to enter

his eyes. He pulled away from me and folded his arms. "Is that why…" His voice cut off. And he rubbed up and down his arms. "Is that the reason we—"

I couldn't stand seeing my mate doubt us for a second. I lifted him off the chair and sat where he'd been with him on my lap. Kian was stiff as a board. "Baby, look at me, please."

He didn't move. "Kian, please," I begged.

I waited and waited and was about to ask again when he slowly turned so he was facing me. I chose to take it as a win that he was even still on my lap. Even though his body language said he'd rather be anywhere else.

"Kian, I didn't even know you were pregnant when I ran up in front of your car," I admitted. "I didn't know when I chose to tell you. I want you. I love you. And our baby will be a great blessing, but I never want you to doubt you're my everything."

I felt his body slowly begin to unclench.

"I will always choose you, Kian. In every life, I'll choose you." I prayed to the Gods he'd believe me because my mate was everything to me.

"You didn't?" Kian whispered.

"I swear, Kian. I had no idea. Besides, I just want you for your body," I teased, sucking at his mating bite.

Kian giggled. "Well, good, because that's the only reason I want you too, for your really big—"

I laughed and kissed him before he could finish his sentence. I pulled back and looked into those gorgeous blue eyes. "I love you, Kian. I know you may not be ready—"

He covered my mouth with his hand. "It's crazy, but I am... I mean I do too. I love you, Gabe." He leaned against my chest and wrapped his hand around my neck.

For the first time in a very, very long time, I was truly content.

17

KIAN

I TILTED MY HEAD TO THE SIDE, TRYING TO FIGURE OUT what was bugging me about the design I was working on.

"Hmm." I tweaked it a little. "That works." I hoped the author thought so. Making book covers was a good, constant income. Plus, it was pretty cool reading a book and knowing I was the one that made the cover.

I sighed and exported the file from Photoshop. I would send it to the author, and if there were any changes, they would let me know.

I was waiting for everything to compile and munching on my popcorn, plantain chips, cheerios, chocolate chips, chocolate-covered raisins, and M&Ms —yum—when there was a knock on the door. I didn't bother moving. I knew they would come in. I really liked the fact that Gabe's family was so close to each other. I really hoped he was right and they liked me. For him.

"Kian." Rhys was apparently my visitor today.

"In the office." I was borrowing Gabe's until the furniture for mine came. We'd spent Saturday shopping, and my furniture should be here any day now.

There were times I thought I should pinch myself to see if this was for real, but then I would look at Gabe and find him already looking at me. Or I'd be waking up snuggled in his arms. Even just making dinner together. It was three days, and I'd never been happier. I cupped my belly, and we were having a little one.

I looked up. "Papa, Daddy, I wish you were here. I wish I could share this life with you." My throat tightened. "I wish you could meet Gabe and your grandbaby."

When the door opened, I looked up and sniffed.

Rhys hurried over to my side of the desk. "Are you okay? Is the baby okay?"

I chuckled. "I'm fine. I guess Gabe told you."

Rhys chuckled and shook his head. "Nope, I could kind of smell it on you," he admitted.

I shook my head and smiled. "That is soo weird."

Rhys laughed and walked over, lowering himself to one of the wingback chairs on the other side of the desk.

"But at least I can tell you now." I saw how happy that made my friend. Again, I couldn't imagine how much it must have eaten him up keeping something like that from me, especially when we shared everything. I noticed him tapping nervously on the arm of the chair.

"I'm not mad, you know," I said. "I can't even imagine what it was like having something that huge as a secret, Rhys. But I'm not upset because you've always been an amazing friend to me, Rhys, and you even brought me here. You trusted me enough. And you gave me Gabe." I tried not to blush.

"Well, you're gonna make me an uncle." Rhys beamed. "Let's call it even stevens."

"Even stevens," I repeated.

Rhys got a mischievous glint in his eyes. "Although I guess we won't be sharing everything. I definitely do not need to hear about you and my brother doing the wild thing."

I burst out laughing. "Wild thing. Really! You're impossible."

"The horizontal mamba." Rhys raised a brow, his lips twitching.

"You're the worst." I rolled my eyes.

"I'm awesome. I even gave you and Gabe three whole days of honeymooning bliss. Totally kept the parents away. You owe me your peanut butter blondie brownies," Rhys said. "Especially since you've ditched me and shacked up with my bro."

I leaned forward. "I told Gabe I should speak to you about that." I lowered my eyes. "I should have told you I was having feelings for Gabe."

"Oh, cut it out!" Rhys snorted. "I love that you're with Gabe. I love that we don't have any more secrets, and I love the fact that you're even more family than you already were."

My heart lightened, and I stretched my hand out, and Rhys took it. "I kinda love all that too."

He squeezed my hands before leaning back. "So what's it like being preggers?" Rhys asked. There was a smile on his face, and I could tell he was happy for me, but it was edged with sadness and a little longing.

"So far not that different. No nausea, but I have fallen asleep twice on Gabe while we watched a movie. He's had to carry me to bed," I admitted. I didn't ask Rhys about what I'd seen. I knew him well enough to know if he wanted to share, he would.

"Bet he's not complaining about that," Rhys said. "I saw him at the office today. He was preening like a peacock. Had a smile on his face the whole day. Everyone is weirded out."

I snorted, but I kind of loved that I made him happier, so much so that people noticed.

"And"—I lifted my bowl—"I've been eating quite a lot. More than usual. It's weird. I can't be more than a week... Maybe I'm just using it as an excuse to eat more."

"Lol, maybe you are, but bear cubs are a little different from humans, so I can totally see the little tyke making you hungry even now."

"He comes out human, right?" My voice was a little panicked even to my ears.

Rhys cackled. My asshole bestie actually bent over laughing.

I grabbed a pen and threw it at him. "You suck." I folded my arms and stuck my lips out.

Rhys finally stopped laughing and straightened. "Yes, we come out human. We don't actually shift for, like, eighteen months. Maybe twelve months for some cubs, later for others."

"Will our kids be able to since I'm—" I hadn't really thought about… Okay, that was a lie. I just hadn't wanted to focus on it. I sighed. "I know Gabe is the head of the den." Rhys nodded. "And our kids will be the next?" He nodded again. "What if they don't get the bear gene?"

Rhys shook his head. "It doesn't really work like that. It would have to be like twice or three times removed for the gene to disappear and even then, not really. From what I understand, the gene can be activated, like if you mate a shifter or something. It's hidden just in case you don't know, and one day, you suddenly shift, and you didn't know you could."

"Mmmm. I guess that makes sense," I said. "That would be so scary."

"Yeah, and it protects us," Rhys added.

"For sure. To be honest, I can't imagine the world knowing. People seem to fear what they can't control."

"Yeah, and scared people react poorly; we all know

this," I murmured. I cradled my bump, suddenly realizing my kid would be born to this and what that meant.

"Let's talk about less stressful topics," he said. "You excited for the baby?"

Rubbing my belly, I nodded. "You know, for a second, I was terrified that was the only reason Gabe —" I sighed.

"Don't even think that. Trust me, I know my brother. He's head over heels in love with you. Besides, he didn't know. He was just out there pining for you. Quite sad, actually. Boohoo, Kian will run if he knows. Ooohh, he'll hate me. I've never seen my older brother so unsure of himself. And it's because of you. The little one is a blessing, and he'll love them—we all will. But now that he's found you, Gabe couldn't exist without you."

"Yeah?" My voice was barely above a whisper.

"Never doubt that." Rhys's voice was firm.

I sniffed and cleared my throat. "I was gonna come over and ask you what to cook for when we have the whole family over. We want to tell them." I groaned, "What if they think I'm not good enough for him, 'cause I'm…you know?"

"Human," Rhys supplied. "It's not a dirty word, Kee, and I would love to hear someone say that in front of Gabe or, worse, Papa." He snorted. "Yeah, I would love to see that."

"And they'll have to get through you," I added.

"And they'll have to get through me," he repeated, grinning at me. Rhys jumped on his feet and stretched his hands out. "Come on. I want to introduce you to someone."

I knew what he meant, so I stood and walked over, slipping my hands in his. "I can't wait to meet him."

We went through the kitchen and opened the double doors that led to the covered patio.

"I love it out here. I still can't believe Gabe has a pool," I said.

"Yeah, he and Austin have one, but you've probably noticed we all kind of pop in and out of each other's houses."

"I love that, you know. You know I always wished I had siblings." I walked over to one of the pool chairs and sat cross-legged.

"I know. Be careful what you wish for 'cause you're stuck with the Hallbjorns now."

I grinned. Yeah, I so wouldn't have it any other way. Rhys took his boxer briefs off till he was standing completely naked in front of me. I guess I finally understood the whole 'not bothered by nudity' thing now.

Rhys knelt, and his body began to shift. Fur appeared, legs extended, ears changed, and suddenly, I was face to face with a large brown bear. Although definitely not as large as Gabe.

The gigantic bear lumbered over to me and stuck its head in my belly. I grinned and wrapped my arms around Rhys's head. And the bear in my arms purred. "You're huge, Rhys. But I'm so glad to meet you."

My best friend purred again, and I rubbed up and down from the top of his head down, and he chuffed happily.

"I love you, Rhys, and your bear is gorgeous. Thanks for introducing him."

Rhys huffed one more time before moving a couple of steps back, and like before, the fur disappeared, and suddenly, my Rhys was standing back in front of me.

He slipped on his underwear before turning to face me. "Lunch?" he asked.

I chuckled and nodded. Apparently, this was my life now.

"I can't eat another bite." I sighed and rubbed my belly. "I wonder why we call it a pasta salad when there's, like, no veggies in it."

"There were cherry tomatoes," he pointed out.

"Yeah, and bacon and tuna and lots and lots of mayo," I added.

"Only needs one veggie to be a salad in my book." Rhys lifted his glass of lemonade and drained it. "Now that I've fed the preggo, let's talk work real quick."

"I cooked," I reminded him.

He waved me off. "I chopped the tomatoes. That was the hardest part."

I snorted. "All right, work. What's up? Did you have any new ideas?"

He shook his head. "Nope, I was wondering if you spoke to Gabe about the designs."

I shook my head and grabbed the plates off the dining table and headed for the kitchen. I heard Rhys follow as I turned the sink on.

"No, uh, not really had the time to." I shrugged. "The moment hasn't presented itself."

"Mmmm…" Rhys murmured.

I knew what that meant. Rhys was saying what he wanted to say without saying it. I turned to face him. "It feels weird now," I finally admitted. "Like I'm taking advantage of the fact we're sleeping together. It's like he didn't say yes before, but I'm expecting him to because—"

"You did the wild thing," Rhys supplied, a teasing grin on his face.

"You're so annoying," I sighed.

"Trust me, Gabe won't say yes just because he's your mate, but remember, you said he didn't approve some of the designs 'cause he was worried you'd leave. Maybe talk to him about that. See whether there's one he actually liked but didn't approve."

"You think that's the only reason he said no?"

"Well, the only way you'll know is if you ask," Rhys pointed out.

"Yeah, I guess you're right."

GABE WALKED INTO OUR BEDROOM—MY belly flipped at the 'our'—and walked over to drop a kiss on my lips. I smiled up at him from where I sat cross-legged on the couch. "How was your day?"

"Good, but I missed you." He cupped my cheek.

"Missed you too," I sighed. "But Rhys came over and kept me company."

"Oh, that's where he got off to," Gabe teased as he straightened.

I looked down at my iPad where I'd been sketching for my Redbubble store. Gabe had ordered me a new tablet to replace the one that I'd dropped on the night of our first kiss.

"I'll get out of these clothes, and you can watch me while I have dinner," Gabe called from the walk-in.

"I waited for you," I replied. "Even though I did demolish almost half of the cookies I baked earlier. But I left some for you."

"This is why you're my favorite person in the whole wide world." Gabe peeked his head out to grin at me but disappeared again.

"So, I was thinking." I nibbled on my lips, but blew out a breath and went on. "Did you pick the logo you liked from the options I submitted?"

Gabe came out, pulling his shirt on. "You don't have to worry about any of that, babe. We can keep the design as it is or even hire someone else to do it."

My stomach clenched, and I felt like I was going to puke. And I knew this had nothing to do with the fact that I was pregnant. "Oh!"

I swallowed, trying to dislodge the sudden tightness in my chest. Gabe was by my side immediately.

"Baby, what's wrong?" he asked, taking my hand in his.

All I could do was shake my head even as tears threatened to fall.

"Kian, what's going on?" Gabe squeezed my hand. "I can tell you're upset."

"Did you hate them that much?" I felt tears roll down my cheeks. "You hate my work."

It felt like my heart was being squeezed slowly.

"What? Why would you say that?" Gabe shook his head.

"You wouldn't even consider my work." I swiped my eyes with the back of my hands. "You're still so set in your ways. How will that work for us?"

Gabe's eyes widened at my words. "Baby, I—" He snapped his mouth shut, and I could see him working through what I'd said.

"I know you like things just so, but we're together now, and I don't know about mates, but in a relationship, we gotta compromise." I sighed. "I have to know that you won't just walk all over me."

"I would never." Gabe's voice was insistent.

"You wouldn't mean to, but sometimes…"

Gabe put his head on my lap and sighed. "I can be

very stubborn," he acknowledged. "I don't do very well with change. I know."

"But I want us to work, and that means we have to be able to—"

"Talk," Gabe finished for me.

"Yeah, and I have to know you're listening, and you'll actually take my side into consideration."

Gabe moved so he was looking me in the eye. "I promise I'll try, but I know I'll mess up. I want you to always call me out on it. Because I want us to work. I want you to be happy."

"I want both of us to be happy," I corrected.

Gabe's lips curved. "Yeah. And I didn't mean I didn't like your work—I meant you don't have to work at all...if you don't want to. I mean, you don't have to."

"Oh." I wasn't really sure what else to say to that. I'd never thought not working was a possibility. But my papa hadn't. Even after Dad had passed away, he'd left us enough that we were taken care of. Even college for me had been set up if I'd wanted to.

But was that what I wanted?

"I like my job, and I always thought it would work even when I had kids 'cause I can work primarily out of my home." I smiled at the memory. "Papa always picked me up from school till I was too old, and he would be at the stove while I did homework at the table and give me homemade cookies and milk as a snack. I want all that with my kids. I think that's why Papa and I were so close because I knew he was there for me always. Even Dad with his job, he was a lawyer, but he still made time for Papa and me." I sighed. "I really wish they could have met you."

"I wish I'd gotten to meet them," Gabe said. "They gave me you, and I will forever be grateful to them for that."

My heart turned over. "I love you," I whispered.

"I love you too"—Gabe beamed at me—"and I swear I will make you happy, Kian, and I'll do my best not to take you for granted."

I pushed my hands through his hair and smiled. "I know you will."

Gabe jumped to his feet and walked back to the closet. He came back out and held up his phone. "I did have one logo I really like. I even saved it on my phone, but it might need a couple of tweaks."

I patted the space beside me. "Show me."

18

GABE

"I STILL CAN'T BELIEVE YOU HAVE A FULL HOSPITAL HERE," Kian said as we pulled up outside the Asheville Medical Center for his first scan.

Even though I'd wanted to take Kian to see Ian the first week we found out he was pregnant, Papa and Kian convinced me we didn't need to go. Papa had checked him out, and everything was going fine, but it was finally his sixth week, and finally, a doctor would be the one to tell me that.

I parked the car in one of the parking spots close to the building that was the medical center for Asheville. "We have to," I reminded him. "Both well-equipped and staffed for our particular needs. The doctors need to take care of both humans and others.

"Like most shifter towns, we make sure our people are well taken care of," I explained. "It's always been like this in packs and dens. The difference now is our den is a town. Usually, if a den member wants to study something that's good for the pack, then we send them to the best college, and so far, ninety percent come home."

"For real?" Kian twisted in his seat to look at me.

I couldn't help it; I stole a quick kiss. "For real," I replied. "Usually only those that find their mates, but most alphas end up bringing their omegas home. Usually, their family too, if possible."

"So living next door to your parents is totally normal around here," Kian said. "I would have loved that."

"Yeah, most people live on the same land as their family or a couple of streets over."

Kian looked over at the medical center. "It doesn't look like any hospital I've ever been to."

"Yeah, we went with the lodge aesthetic, as you can see. Fits with the surrounding mountains, don't you think?"

"It definitely does," he said.

"We're one of the best in the rural hospitals in the northwest."

"You sound very proud of that," Kian said.

"I am," I admitted. "Our hospital has forty beds with everything from a critical care facility, a state-of-the-art diagnostic imaging service, our very own lab, and of course a state-of-the-art birth center."

"Wow," he said.

"You'll be well taken care of," I reassured him.

"I know," he teased. "You'd never let any less happen."

"You know it. Only the very best care for my mate."

Kian slipped his hand in mine and squeezed.

"I love hearing the history of our town," Kian said.

I'd never get tired of hearing him say *our*.

"Well, here is your history for the day," I said. "This hospital was built eight years ago, but we've had our own medical center for over sixty years." I turned around. "If you look behind you—actually, hold on." I turned the car off and jumped out, hurrying over to his side and opening the door for him. I helped him out and shut the door. Then turned him around. "Over there." I pointed across the street where the old hospital still stood. "It's now something of a haven for omegas and teens that need help."

"Wow, that's amazing. I want to volunteer."

And that was why he was the best thing that had ever happened to me. "You'll make a perfect alpha mate."

"I can't believe there are abused omegas. I thought mates couldn't hurt each other…"

I squeezed him to my side. "They can't, but not all matings are fated. Just like humans, we have people who take what isn't theirs. But they all know they're safe in Asheville."

"I kind of love you a lot right now." Kian smiled softly up at me.

"I kind of love you a lot too," I said back to him. "Now come on, let's go meet our little pumpkin."

Kian grinned. "Yeah, let's."

We walked hand in hand to the entrance, and the admissions clerk at the desk smiled at me. "Mr. Hallbjǫrn, welcome. We are so excited to have you. Congratulations."

"Thank you, Francine." I smiled and waved. She was a sister of Thomas, who worked on the ranch.

"Thanks, Francine. We're here to see Dr. Matthews?"

"You know the way. He's expecting you." She nodded in the direction of his office.

I led Kian through to the hallways to Dr. Matthews's office. I knew my way around the hospital since I'd been involved from planning to completion.

I knocked on the doc's door and was told to enter.

Ian stood on our entry and came over. "Gabe." He pulled me in for a hug.

"Ian," I said as I hugged him back. When we stepped away, I pulled Kian in front of me. "This is my wonderful mate, Kian." Even I heard the pride in my voice.

"Nice to meet you, Kian." Ian held his hand out to my mate after looking to me for permission.

"You too, Dr. Matthews. Gabe has said wonderful things about you."

"Please call me Ian," he said to my mate. His eyes on Kian's belly narrowed, but before I could ask, the look was gone. "And I would hope so since we've been friends since we were cubs." Ian nudged me. "Great Urs bless your mating."

"Thanks, Ian." I smiled at my old friend.

"Come on." He opened the door for us. "Let's get to the checkup first. Then you can ask whatever questions you have."

I held my mate's hand as we moved out of the office to a room across from it. This one had an exam table and an ultrasound device. There were two large TVs, one tilted over the bed and one across from the chair that was clearly for the doc, even though the ultrasound machine had one.

Ian went over to the sink and washed his hands. "Please get up on the exam table, Kian. I'm sure your strapping mate can help you."

"My pleasure." I lifted him up to the table. And kissed him. "I love you, Kian." My mate leaned into my chest, his legs dangling off the table.

"I love you too, Gabe," Kian whispered, "and I can't wait to share everything with you, from the quiet nights at home in front of the TV to long, stay-awake-all-nights with the kids teething, to vacations in Disneyland or wherever else. Just with you."

Kian didn't know what his words meant to me. It had been five amazing weeks with him. I'd found myself leaving work early because I had someone to come home to. I didn't want to miss any moment of our lives I didn't have to.

"Okay, lovebirds, let's meet your little ones." I turned to my friend, and he had a knowing smile on his face.

"How's Adam and the kids?" I asked.

"Good, Adam just completed the designs for a new estate in Billings. His first solo project." I didn't miss the pride in his voice for his mate. "The two of you should come over for dinner."

I looked over at Kian and raised a brow. "We'd love to," my mate replied for both of us.

"You heard the boss. We'd love to," I said.

Ian laughed as he slipped on gloves and took a seat on the stool beside the bed. "Looks like you've already figured out how mated life works."

Kian snorted. "He's a fast learner," he teased.

"Always has been," Ian said. "Please lift your T-shirt, Kian."

My mate did as he was asked. And I couldn't help the smile that appeared on my face when I saw the small mound that was my mate's belly. Somewhere deep down in a very primitive place, I couldn't stop the glow of satisfaction at the obvious changes in my mate's body that showed his pregnancy. I was fertile. Kian was carrying my seed in his belly. There was a very heady feeling knowing I was responsible for that change.

Kian looked up at me, and we shared a smile, and he slipped his hand into mine.

"Ready?" Ian asked.

We grinned and nodded. "Yup. Let's get this show on the road," Kian said.

"Well, you heard the boss," I said to Ian.

Ian chuckled and squirted the gel on Kian's stomach. My mate's grip on my hand tightened. I followed all of Ian's movements with my eyes. Until an image appeared on the monitor in front of him.

The quiet seemed to stretch out, and Kian and I exchanged a look. My heart raced, and Kian squeezed my hand so hard I thought he would manage to break a bone in there. I could hear his racing heartbeat, and there was a sour undertone to his scent that told me he was as scared as I was. The narrow-eyed look Ian had given Kian when they were first introduced flashed into my head.

"That's what I thought," Ian finally spoke, breaking the silence. He looked at us, and his dark eyes danced, and some of the tightness around my chest loosened. That wasn't a bad look.

"Congratulations, you two." Ian grinned. "Just what I thought. You're having twins."

My mouth dropped, and Kian's eyes widened, and his head swiveled to Ian. "What!" he said. "Are you sure?"

"Pretty sure," Ian replied, chuckling. "Watch the monitor," he urged.

Suddenly, the blurry image became astonishingly clear and in 3D.

"That's a baby," I whispered, amazement in my

voice even though I knew my mate was pregnant. I hadn't expected everything to be so recognizable, and certainly not a tiny face.

"Oh, he's so…so beautiful," Kian said shakily.

I closed a hand over his. "Are we having a boy?"

"Do you want to know?" Ian checked.

"Isn't it too soon?" Kian asked.

"Not at all. With the pregnancy being over seven weeks along according to the measurements and full-term being twenty-six weeks, it should be no problem."

"Twenty-six!" Kian gasped, his eyes meeting mine.

"Yeah, your due date should be around the end of September, early October," Ian replied.

"Not forty weeks?" Kian checked.

"Ahh, I see the confusion." Ian nodded. "Bear cubs gestate for a shorter amount of time between five to seven months. Being human, from experience, it falls in the five- to six-month space."

"And they'll be okay?" Kian whispered.

"Completely fine. Your body is perfectly capable of baking them, but you might have to slow down as time goes on."

Kian nodded. "I can do that as long as they're fine." His voice was still shaky, and I squeezed his hand in support. "And yes, I think we'd like to know," he said.

Ian grinned before turning back to the monitor. "This one is a boy."

"It's a little difficult to be sure with the babies in this

position, but I'm almost certain the other is also a boy," Ian said.

"Twins. Boys." Kian sounded awe struck.

"Wow." I was still stunned, and my hand tightened on Kian's, my thumb and forefinger gently massaging his wrist. I faced the TV instead of the smaller monitor Ian had been using, and I was spellbound, my attention completely held by the images of my sons in perfect HD.

"Are they healthy?" Kian pressed anxiously.

"Perfectly," Ian said. The reassurance he received seemed to ease his concern. "Don't worry about anything, although I will suggest adding an extra five hundred calories to your diet and getting plenty of rest."

Happiness, pride, and a fierce feeling of protective-ness towards my mate and our babies overwhelmed me.

"We need to start getting stuff together now," Kian whispered.

I nodded, still a little dazed.

"The baby store in town has some wonderful selec-tions, and of course, Cubs carries a wide range of options," Ian chimed in with the suggestion. Then he asked, "Would the two of you like images...a video of the ultrasound?"

We said yes in unison, and the three of us laughed.

"I'll get this on a USB for you and print out the images while you get cleaned up," Ian said.

I used the tissue provided to wipe the gel, then helped my mate sit up. I kissed him tenderly, pouring all the emotions rioting through my body into it. Kian sighed and wrapped his hand around my waist.

When we pulled back, I traced his kiss-stung lips, and his beautiful blue eyes darkened. I would never get tired of the telling dilation of his pupils and the slight audible catch of breath in his throat when I lifted my hand to the nape of his neck.

"How would you feel about a date with your baby daddy?"

"What's the plural of baby daddy?" he teased.

"Babies daddies?" I supplied.

"I think that means there's two of you, not two babies," Kian said. Gods, I loved seeing him radiate happiness, and he did.

"Nope, not two, just me. Got you all knocked up by myself," I growled. "You're all mine."

"Caveman," Kian snorted even as his heart sped up at my words.

"You love my caveman ways," I teased, waggling my brows.

"Mmm, I think I forgot what those are. You might have to remind me," Kian whispered, nipping my lobe.

I barely swallowed my growl, and if Ian hadn't snorted, interrupting us, I would have ravished my mate. "Oh, the honeymoon phase, although I suppose with mates that never ends," he teased. "Get a room, you two. Preferably not this one," he added, giving me a pointed look.

I shrugged and helped Kian off the exam table. "Can't make any promises."

Kian elbowed me in my side. "Ignore him." It was followed by an eye roll.

We took the USB and images and left the hospital on a happiness high like never before.

"OKAY." Kian held up a sailor outfit. "This. This is the last one. Can you imagine a picture with two chubby little sailors?"

I shook my head and smiled indulgently at my mate. We'd been at the store almost forty-five minutes. Kian had chosen Cubs over the baby store, figuring things would be way more affordable there. I didn't have to the heart to tell him that he couldn't spend enough to put a dent in the Hallbjǫrn fortune in one lifetime.

So I followed him and made the appropriate sounds at every cute outfit he held up and every tiny little bootie he clasped against his chest. I just loved seeing him so happy.

"I want a lot of pictures of them matching. I just know once they're older, they won't let me do that." I nodded along because I was just basking in my mate's excitement and mine too.

"Twins." I couldn't believe it. Our tiny family was about to double, and I knew my papa, dad, and siblings would be just as excited as I was.

Kian stopped when we got to the stroller aisle. "I think I wanna do a little research before we get one. I'll probably need something all-terrain and sturdy." He shook his head. "How is this my life?"

If I didn't hear the excitement in his voice or see it on his face, I'd be worried. But I wasn't.

"I have an idea for the crib," I said. "Unless you have one in mind."

Kian walked around the cart and hugged my side. "You do?"

"Yeah, there are a lot of artisans in town, and I'd like to order a custom-made crib for our little guys."

Kian sighed. "They're gonna be so lucky having you as their dad."

"Having us," I said.

"Yeah," he murmured. "You know"—Kian's voice was barely above a whisper—"there's days I wake up, and for a split second, I'm terrified this will all be a dream. And I'll be all alone again."

I turned so I could hug my mate to me. "I know the feeling," I admitted. "There's days I wake up scared that you've left or, worse, you never came." I breathed in my mate's scent, reminding myself he was here, he was real, and he was mine.

"Can't get rid of me." He gave me an impish smile, and I couldn't help myself. I claimed his lips in a slow, sensual kiss that sent a shiver of reaction traveling down his body.

Kian pulled back, his eyes heavy-lidded. "If we don't want to give them a show in the baby aisle of the grocery store, I suggest we get out of here."

"Good idea," I whispered to my mate and kept a hold of his hand as I grabbed the cart with the other and pushed it in the direction of the checkout.

Walking through the store, a few people stopped to greet us and offer their congratulations for our mating. My mate handled it like a pro; he was warm and welcoming.

When we got to the checkout, there were a couple of people ahead of us in line. Most of the cashiers had lines. Not that it surprised me being a Friday, but I didn't mind waiting. I'd taken the day off, and Bailey knew to call Rhys with any issues that might arise today.

"Did you remember to get everything delivered for the barbecue on Sunday?" Kian whispered up at me. "Rhys, Jon, and I were here two days ago, but you said you'd have all the meat delivered."

I kissed the side of his head. "I did, babe. Should be delivered this evening."

"Okay, good. I gotta season the ribs and everything. I don't wanna have to do it on Sunday. That's for the sides." Kian sounded a little stressed. "And the dessert, maybe I shouldn't have asked Graham to make it. We're hosting. Would it be cheating having a pastry chef make them?"

I sighed, trying to remember why the hell I'd agreed to this party. It was stressing my mate out. But he and Rhys had gotten it in their heads, and now here we were. "Everything will work out just fine, and if it doesn't, well, fine. We can always offer them cereal."

Kian elbowed me. "Don't even put that in the air."

I was about to reply when I heard it. "Human, can you believe it! It's a damn shame diluting the Hallbjǫrn line." It was a female voice.

"I know! Damn shame. He was always so damn responsible. A very fine leader. You'd think he'd have more sense than that. If I were him, I would find a good strong omega to—" This time, it was a man that spoke.

Kian's body physically collapsed in on itself. I spun around and walked right over to the two I knew were speaking. I knew this because every eye was on them.

My bear was right at the surface. I recognized the older man; his brother Rob was on the town council. And the other was a middle-aged woman I couldn't place. Not that I cared who they were. "I am taking a moment before someone gets their throats ripped out," I growled.

They both took a step back, and I basked in the fear they felt. For the first time in a long time, I wasn't the head of my den—I was a man protecting his mate.

"You will watch what you say about my mate." I

narrowed my eyes at them. "You will never say anything that hurts him, or there will be consequences." I made sure to keep my voice even, but my claws dug into my fingers. "Is that clear?"

They nodded.

"Is that clear?" I growled.

"Yeah," she said.

"Yes. Yes," he said.

"Now, I believe you owe my mate an apology." I walked over and stood behind Kian.

"Alpha mate, please accept my apology," the woman said.

"I apologize for the pain caused by my words," the man, Brian, said. They both presented their necks to Kian.

My mate inclined his head, but I could feel the tension in his body. Kian whispered, "Can we please leave?"

I didn't even look at anyone; I simply took his hand and walked him out of the store. When we were beside the car, I pulled him into my arms and held him tight.

Kian sobbed in my arms, and I simply held him until he was done.

"You're perfect, baby. Absolutely perfect," I whispered.

And I would deal with anyone that said otherwise about my mate. And I made a promise to myself to remind him of it every day.

19

KIAN

"This is all your fault," I growled and pushed my mate away again as he tried nibbling on my neck. "Shoo. Go away. Go away and do something." I batted him away. "You made me burn the roux. I gotta start over. I can't serve crappy mac and cheese—it's like the easiest meal. And I still need to make the pasta salad."

I'd precooked so much pasta. Penne for Reese's salad and macaroni for mine.

"You don't have to stress so much." Gabe tried again, for what felt like the fiftieth time, but he didn't get it. "You already made skewers and seasoned the ribs, chicken drumsticks, wings, and burger meat. Which I had to roll out by hand even though we have a whole factory that does just that," he grumbled.

I ignored the last part. I'd wanted to season it the way Dad did. "Yeah, and the ribs and pulled pork for the slow cooker are already cooking."

He gave me a look that I recognized meant a lecture was in my future. I preempted this by reminding him of what I'd said when I'd woken up at five a.m. to get everything started. "It's just for those that want a different taste. Not just grilled. You did remind Graham about getting the buns and desserts here on time, right?"

Gabe looked like he was about to tell me to slow down again, but he must have read something on my face because instead, he simply replied, "Yes. And he's bringing beer too. The brewery is his new project."

"Thank you." I blew out a breath. "I know you don't understand, but I really want this day to be perfect."

I really didn't need to give anyone another reason not to like me. I knew Gabe would growl at anybody that looked at me sideways, but I didn't want that. This was my new town, my new home, and my job was to support Gabe, not cause more problems for him.

"I just think you're doing way too much, babe," Gabe said from where he hovered on the other side of the island. "You are pregnant, Kian. You should be taking it easy. My family won't mind burgers and hotdogs."

"Ian said I was fine, and I feel well, strong and well-rested. Plus, I had a really hearty breakfast," I reminded him. Gabe had made oatmeal with cinnamon and brown sugar topped with blueberries and bananas. And he'd gone overboard, making way more than one person could eat.

"And your daily dose of Vitamin G." He leered playfully at me. I groaned and Gabe winked at me.

"That was bad. Like, really, just bad." Still, I couldn't stop my lips from twitching.

"Made you smile, though, didn't I?" Gabe pointed out, seemingly pleased by the fact.

"It did. Now shoo. I need to get this mac and cheese done and ready to go in the oven. And there's like four pans." I sighed. "Will that be enough?" Gahhh! I could just see stuff running out and everyone thinking I was a horrible host or couldn't take care of my mate. I could, and I would prove it. I might not sprout fur, but Gabe was mine, and this was our home. I would show them I could be his alpha mate.

Gabe came around and pulled me back into his body. "Stop fretting, baby, please."

I kept stirring my roux so the flour-and-butter mix didn't burn again. "They already think I'm not good enough. If I serve them burned or tasteless food, it'll just make everyone think I can't take care of you. That you can do better."

"I should have gutted them," Gabe growled. I knew who *them* was. "We take care of each other, don't we, baby? Me and you, we're partners, right?"

I sniffed but nodded. My stubborn mate was learning and gave me new reasons to love him daily.

"And trust me, Kian, I couldn't do better because you're the best thing that's ever happened to me," Gabe whispered.

"You're the best thing that happened to me too." My body sagged against his.

"Baby, if that's why we're having this party, then we can cancel," Gabe said.

I shook my head and straightened my spine. "No, I actually want to host everyone. Your parents had us over. Rhys too, and I want to have them here."

"Well, as long as that's the only reason why." I didn't miss the concern in my mate's tone.

And I was going to reassure him again when Rhys called out, "Innocent eyes approaching. Cover all naughty bits."

Gabe and I snorted as we heard footsteps approach. He didn't move from his position behind me even while I folded cheese into my roux. And holy crap, I'd never made this much food in my life.

Still, my mac and cheese recipe had never failed me.

"I knew it. You guys can't keep your hands off each other." He shoved Gabe away. "Go do something. We've got cooking to do."

Gabe sighed. "Baby, get him. He's picking on me."

I turned the heat down and turned to look at my mate and could barely keep a straight face at the pout he wore. It was adorable on such a big, muscled man.

I stood next to Rhys and bumped his hip. "Omega solidarity."

Gabe grabbed his heart dramatically. "Oh, the betrayal. Cuts so deep."

I rolled my eyes and shared a grin with Rhys.

"I think he's bored," Rhys mused.

"I agree." I nodded.

"We should put him to work. Put all those muscles to good use," Rhys added like Gabe wasn't there.

"We should." I nodded to my friend, even though I wasn't sure what he meant. But I loved the brothers' relationship. And sure, Rhys and I were great. But I kind of wanted a good relationship with all of them.

This was another reason why I wanted to have the party. I knew Gabe would fight for me, but I didn't want him to have to, at least not with his family. I wanted to be good with all of them. I wanted them to feel welcome in our home like they always had when it was just Gabe.

So far none of them had said a bad word. Jon and Stefan hosted us after we'd gotten mated, and they'd seemed genuinely happy for us. All his brothers had been genuinely welcoming. I'd also spent time with Austin and Hunter. The two of them joined us for dinner quite often since they had to talk about den business with Gabe.

Then there was Graham. He'd always been very nice to me, but he was also very busy. Even Jonathan tried to get him to slow down. But today, I would be meeting Gabe's grandparents. They'd arrived yesterday. This had to go well.

The thought of hearing them say what those people in the store had... I shooed off the thought. It wouldn't happen because I would be above reproach.

Gabe came in with another large slow cooker. I didn't even know they made bigger-sized versions till I came to Asheville. But Rhys was making baked beans with a family recipe, which he'd shared with me. And it was something so small, but I loved it. I knew how seriously families took stuff like that, and he gave it to me.

I was taking the mac off the stove when Gabe came back in. I must have missed him leaving the last time. "You have a slushie and popcorn machine."

"Yup," I grinned.

Gabe shook his head and looked at Rhys. "Stop enabling him. You know he doesn't have to do this much."

Rhys shrugged as he put together a penne pasta salad with mayo and salad dressing, eggs, boiled and mashed sausage, tuna, crushed bacon, diced red bell peppers, and pickles. "I think it's great. The family is growing. New traditions will be added. Who knows? This could be one of many of Kian's Fourth of July parties."

"I like the sound of that. So mote it be," I declared. Before Gabe could leave, I reminded him to set up the table outside and grab the baskets from the pantry with all the supplies.

Gabe groaned. "I should have gone over to Austin's." He managed a put-upon sigh before leaving us there. Rhys and I shared a look before getting back to work.

When the mac and cheese was done and topped

with breadcrumbs and bacon and put in the oven, I found myself whispering to my God and my parents not to let this go wrong. Oh, and dear lord, I really hoped no one minded that the coleslaw was store-bought. I would totally blame Rhys if they did.

I rolled my shoulders before grabbing the ingredients to make my own burger sauce. It was actually my dad's, but I hoped they'd like it. A voice that sounded a lot like Gabe's whispered, *If they don't, they can fuck off.*

I chuckled lightly. My mate was right. There was only so much I could do.

EVERYTHING SEEMED to be going great, Gabe manned one grill and Hunter had the other. My mate was very proud of his grills; they even had their own covered gazebo space.

I still couldn't believe that we had two in our backyard.

I brought out yet another tray of mac and cheese and couldn't help preening at the fact everyone seemed to be enjoying it. In fact, everything looked like it was going well.

I put the tray of mac and cheese down on the long table and checked all the other trays to make sure nothing needed to be refilled. Hands were placed on my shoulder. I turned around and found Jon.

"Everything is perfect. Take a seat, relax." He moved

me towards where the tables and chairs had been set up. Towards Gabe's grandparents, who I'd managed to only greet and dip earlier.

I tried not to drag my feet, but I was definitely taking smaller steps.

"They don't bite," Jon whispered in my ears and squeezed my shoulder.

Easy for him to say. He was gorgeous and a bear. And really super nice.

"Trust me," Jon said, and we didn't stop until we were in the circle made up of solid log furniture with cushions.

"Kian!" A beautiful older woman with medium-length silver-grey hair got on her feet, arms stretched out for a hug. "You've been so busy. Come sit with us. Tell us about yourself."

Jonathan gave me a small push, and I was wrapped up in surprisingly strong arms, then led to one of the empty seats. She sat beside me.

"This is a lovely party," Gabe's grandpa said.

"Thank you, sir," I said.

"Sir!" He shook his head, "Please call me Frederic. And the gorgeous woman that has you in a death grip is my beautiful mate Sofia."

"Hi." I waved, then realized how dorky that was and put my hands between my thighs. "It's nice to meet you both properly."

"You too, son," Sofia said. "I was sorry to hear about

your parents." She hugged me to her, and my chest tightened. "Thank you."

"I know nothing can ever fill that hole, but you've got us now, and I know we're a loud bunch, but we always show up for family, and that's what you are now."

Tension drained from my body, even as my eyes smarted, tears threatening.

"Oh, dear boy." Sofia clucked her tongue.

Gabe appeared and squatted beside me. "You okay, baby?"

"I'm fine. You didn't have to come," I told him as he took my hand in his.

"Of course he did," Frederic interjected, "as any good mate should. But my grandson should also know we'd never do anything to hurt his mate." His tone was chiding.

"His pregnant mate," Sofia added, and I looked over and saw her grinning.

"I know, Pops, but you know…" Gabe's shoulder lifted and dropped.

"I do," Frederic acknowledged, patting Gabe on his shoulder.

"How are you feeling?" Sofia asked. "I hope my grandson is taking good care of you." She clapped; excitement rolled off her. "I can't wait to be a great-grandma."

"You look too young to be anyone's great-grandma," I told her.

"Oh, you're too kind, son." She smiled. "I love my grandkids, but they're too old. More great-grandkids, that's what I need to keep me young."

"We have a video, of the ultrasound," I clarified. "Would you like to see it?"

Gabe clapped. "That's a great idea. We have a surprise for you guys."

"I would love to," Sofia replied, her hands clasped to her chest.

"Me too," Jon chimed in. "If I had known, I would have come over the moment you got back from the doctor's."

"We know, Papa," Gabe said. "But we wanted to share the surprise with everyone at the same time."

My mate looked like the cat that ate the canary, bursting with excitement.

"Surprise? What surprise?" Jonathan looked between us like he thought he'd read the answers on our faces.

"A very good one." Gabe grinned. I moved to stand, but he patted my shoulder, keeping me seated. "I'll grab the laptop. Sit, babe."

I rolled my eyes and watched him until he disappeared into the house.

"My grandson is very lucky," Sofia murmured.

Heat suffused my cheeks. "I'm the lucky one," I assured her.

"Bet he's driving you crazy," Jonathan said.

I groaned, nodding. "You can say that again." But as

much as I complained, I really wouldn't have it any other way.

Stefan nipped Jon's shoulder, and I saw his body melt. "Is that a complaint?" Stefan asked, brow raised.

I could imagine Gabe and me, years from now, watching our kids with their own mates.

Gabe came back with the laptop and put it on my lap. "Why don't you do the honors, babe?" He handed me the USB.

We shared a smile as I opened the laptop. I folded it over so it was a tablet and put the USB in, then opened it up. I couldn't help it. I stroked the screen as our babies appeared.

"Oh my." Sofia's voice caught, and I lifted my eyes to meet hers.

"I want a look too," Jonathan said.

I smiled and handed it to Sofia. "How about we pass it down the line," I suggested. Of course, no one listened. They all crowded behind her to get a peek.

"Kian and I are having twins." The pride was unmistakable in Gabe's voice.

I used the back of my hand to smack him. "You could have let them be surprised."

"Twins," Jonathan and Rhys gasped. My best friend must have slipped out of the pool without me noticing.

There was a lot of excited chatter that followed as the whole family congratulated us.

Stefan came over and pulled Gabe into a hug. Then he held his hand out for me. "You too, son."

I burrowed into Stefan's broad chest. Gabe's dad was taller, broader, and more muscled than he was. Truth was, neither he nor Jon looked old enough to have kids in their mid-thirties.

"I gotta call my brother. He gloated last year when Coop and Nicole had their little one," Stefan said. "Now I get two for one."

"Don't antagonize your brother," Frederic said, even though his lips twitched.

Jonathan snorted and pushed his mate aside. "Our grandbabies are not coupons." He hugged me first, then Gabe. Soon we were enveloped in hugs from the whole family.

Until Rhys pulled me out of the fray. "I told you everything would be fine." My best friend and I began strolling around the yard.

"Was I that obvious?" I sighed.

"Not really, but I've kinda know you forever. I could tell you were anxious earlier, but I figured telling you not to worry wouldn't do any good."

"You know me so well," I said, leaning against him.

We were quiet as we walked until Rhys came to a stop. We faced each other, and he pulled me in for a solo hug this time. "Congratulations, Kee. I'm so happy for you."

"You know I could never thank you enough, right?"

Rhys's lip lifted at the side, a small smile appearing. "Mmm, I need to get your mate to buy me something crazy big and expensive."

I laughed and linked our arms and got us moving. "You absolutely should."

"Without you, I definitely wouldn't be here right now." I bumped his hip, and he bumped mine right back. We grinned, sharing a smile. I knew Rhys was happy for me, but the longing on his face was unmistakable. I couldn't imagine what it was like knowing there was this one perfect person for you out there and not knowing when you'd meet them.

"I know you'll find your person, Rhys," I whispered, stopping before we made it back to the family. "And he'll be amazing because you deserve the absolute best."

He held my gaze, his eyes glistening, and he swallowed before saying, "Promise?"

"Promise."

"Next time someone talks smack to you, let me know. I'll fight them," Rhys said.

I snort-laughed. "I know you will."

"What's this about a fight?" Hunter slipped between us, linking each of our arms through his.

"It's nothing—"

"Ignore him," Rhys interrupted me. "I can't believe you've not heard."

We were back with the family, and I so didn't want them to hear this. Didn't even need the thought crossing their mind.

"Gabe handled it," I tried.

"I wish I could have really handled it," Gabe growled. I sighed and slipped out of Hunter's arm and went over to my mate. He immediately pulled me down to his lap.

"What's this?" Stefan asked.

"Nothing," I tried again.

"Nope, ignore him." Rhys shushed me. "I heard that Brian Miller said we're diluting the bloodline."

Sofia growled. "Not this shit again. That's what they said when Frederic's great-grandparents wanted to mate. That's how Asheville and a lot of other shifter towns exist. Can't believe that shit is going on today. Here." She was fuming.

"Proud of you, son. I would have punched him," Stefan simply said.

This was my family. I should have trusted them. And I would from now on because all of Gabe's family looked like they were out for blood.

I really hoped my parents could see that I was okay. Even though I wished they could have met their grand-babies, I knew my kids would be so loved.

20

GABE

"Get it away from me now." My mate covered his mouth and ran towards the guest bathroom.

I sighed and cleaned the eggs and steak out. My mate had looked green, but even though I wanted to follow after him, I knew better. If he came back and all of this was still here, we would be doing a replay of this scene. So I got everything in the bin and loaded the dishwasher. I also emptied the trash bag and took it out. Kian's sense of smell had become almost as good as mine.

When I walked back into the kitchen, I found my mate munching on the only thing that he could stomach at the moment. It was an apple cinnamon muffin that Graham had made for him. He'd been dropping it off almost daily for Kian, and my mate loved it. Apparently, it was made with oat flour, which

Kian could stand, but even the sight of oatmeal had him gagging.

"Do I need to ask Graham to drop off more muffins?" I asked.

Kian stopped with the muffin halfway to his mouth, "Are you saying I'm eating too much? Are you calling me greedy?"

I backed away with my hands in the air. Ooh, no, I knew a minefield when I saw one. "Of course not, baby. I'm just happy you can keep anything down."

Kian sighed. "Oh. Okay." He took another bite of his treat and chewed slowly, then swallowed before speaking. "I thought morning sickness was supposed to be in the first trimester, not over halfway through. Kneeling down right now feels like a gymnastic move."

I closed the space between us, walking over to him. "You're beautiful, baby," I reassured him. And he was. Even with carrying twins, my mate's belly was surprisingly small. Not that I'd have minded if it weren't. Kian would always be stunning to me. Hell, I'd even been worried. I still was. Over the last month, he could barely keep anything down. Ian had checked him out and said he was okay, but he couldn't lose any more weight. Which was why the muffins from Graham were a blessing. My mate's diet consisted of very bland chicken or tomato soup or a peanut-butter-and-jelly sandwich. "I'll stay home. It's Friday. Rhys can deal with anything that comes up in the office."

"No, it's fine." Kian rested his forehead on my chest. "I'll get back in bed and flip through all our TV streaming sites. There must be something to watch."

"You sure? I won't mind being your TV-show buddy." I rubbed up and down his back. "And I can help if you need to hurry to the bathroom."

"I'm fine," Kian said. "Besides, I'm only twelve weeks. I can't have you waiting on me every day for the next fourteen."

"Why not, baby?" I pulled back so I could see his face. Kian looked wiped. "It's not only my job but my honor and pleasure to look after you."

"I know, but I'm fine," Kian said, brushing my brow until I had no choice but to stop frowning. "My stomach's settled. At least the one thing this morning sickness is doing correctly is sticking to morning."

"Are you sure?" My bear and I were really in protection mode.

"I am. Besides, Jonathan is coming to keep me company today," Kian informed me. "We're going to do some shopping online."

"I could work from the home office," I said. "I'll be close by…"

Kian sighed and pushed out of my arms. "I'm pregnant, not sick, Gabe. I can take care of myself," he snapped. On the heels of that, Kian sniffed. "I'm sorry. I didn't mean to be short with you."

"I know, love." I kissed him quickly and backed

away before I said or did something else to annoy him. "Do you need me to help you upstairs?" I checked. Kian shot me a narrow-eyed look. "Got it. Pregnant, not sick."

I grabbed my laptop bag and was out of the door before my mate found something else I said annoying. According to my dad and Bailey, I should get used to it, especially with twins. It had to be double the hormones.

MY PAPA HAD STOPPED REPLYING to my messages. But I was just checking on my mate. I'd spoken to him twice already today, but I couldn't help worrying. My bear and I wanted to protect our mate and cubs.

Gabe: Did he have lunch? Did he like the flowers?

Papa: Your mate is fine, son. And he loved the flowers. He's also had lunch. Grilled cheese. And now he's working.

My papa knew me well and what questions I'd ask, so he'd answered all of them. And I was happy to see we'd added one more option to his food choices.

Gabe: How did you manage that?

Papa: He wanted it really charred.

I definitely didn't understand pregnancy cravings, but all my bear and I cared about was our mate's happiness.

Gabe: Thanks for being there, Papa.

I got an eye roll emoji followed by,

Papa: Silly cub. Of course I'm here. Now get back to work, and don't worry about your mate.

Now that I knew my mate was okay, I managed to get some work done. But like most days recently, I ended up shopping for baby stuff. Between my brothers, my parents, my grandparents and friends in town, our kids already had way too much.

It occurred to me I should check on the cribs I'd commissioned instead of ordering any more items we probably already had. I couldn't wait to see them. I knew exactly what I wanted, and after running what crib Kian wanted by him, my friend Dom, who had a high-end carpentry business that specialized in custom pieces, was bringing my vision to life. He'd been fully booked already, but he'd agreed to make them for me. They would look perfect in the nursery, which was already done, just waiting for the cots.

I dialed Dom and waited. Usually, he took a while

to get to his phone, especially while he was in his workshop.

"Gabe. How you doing?" Dom, ever cheerful, asked.

"Good! Good! You? How's Jay and the little one?" I asked.

"Fantastic, my mate is a saint," Dom said. "Even though they never tell you, you never truly have a clean house ever again or sleep in past nine."

I chuckled. "Looking forward to it."

"I bet. I bet," Dom said. "And I know you're calling for the cribs. They should be ready before the end of the month."

"Thanks for doing this, Dom. I really appreciate it," I said. "I know Kian will feel better when the cribs are in the nursery. He's been—"

Dom laughed. "Oh, I know. Trust me, but hey, we can never imagine what they're going through. Although there were days I was sure he was keeping himself from gutting me, I irritated him so much."

"I know how that feels." I shook my head thinking about it. "Some days, I get a super clingy Kian. Others everything annoys him."

"Some days?" Dom snorted. "Lucky you, mine could go from minute to minute."

He wasn't wrong. "But we wouldn't have it any other way," I pointed out. I would take my mate cranky and annoyed by me, just as I did when he curled into my body and fell asleep on my chest.

"You said it, brother," Dom agreed.

We chatted a little more before finally getting off the phone. By the time it was time to go home, I wondered which Kian I would return to, but it didn't really matter because whichever one, I'd missed him. And I couldn't wait to get home.

21

KIAN

"CAN'T WE JUST STAY HOME?" I SIGHED, RUBBING MY back as Rhys helped me into his car. Being twenty-two weeks along, I definitely wasn't in the mood to go traipse around from store to store. Just the thought of shopping anywhere but online sounded like a chore currently.

"Nope, you promised me a day out and lunch, and that's what we're doing," he said before closing the door and walking around to the driver's side.

When he got in the car, I looked over at him and pushed my lips out. "Please, Rhys! We can totally order in from Rosso and watch TV."

Rhys shook his head. "Nope." I saw the stubborn look on his face, and I knew I wasn't getting out of this.

"You look like your brother when you have that obstinate look on your face," I said and stuck my tongue out at him.

"I see the way you look at my brother. That means you think I'm gorgeous." Rhys stuck his tongue out right back at me.

I rolled my eyes and buckled up.

"Don't worry," Rhys said as we got moving, "you'll like this."

"I better, or no baby time for you," I threatened.

Rhys gasped dramatically. "That's low." He glanced my way, and I made sure to keep a straight face. "You wouldn't."

I grinned at him. "I so would. No Uncle Rhys time for you."

"Stop whining. You're gonna enjoy this." Rhys huffed. "Babies, remember how mean your papa was to your Uncle Rhys."

I laughed again. "Oh, don't sulk. You're going to be these babies' uncle and godfather."

"What?" Rhys's hand tightened around the steering wheel. He took his eyes off the road for a second, and I saw the emotion there.

"Me, really?" His voice was choked. "I thought it had to be a friend since I'm the uncle."

"You are my friend, though, Rhys," I reminded him. "And you're my brother, so I don't know who else I would possibly choose to be our babies' godfather."

"You're so sappy," he sniffed.

I also had to wipe tears from my eyes. And I found myself thanking everything for whoever had paired Rhys and me up as roommates.

We left the ranch, but instead of going right towards town, we went left, towards the mountains. "I thought we were going shopping."

"I never said we were. You assumed. I didn't correct you," Rhys corrected me.

"So where are we going?"

"Can you just chill and wait for your surprise!" Rhys smirked at me. Clearly, he was pleased with himself.

"This better be good," I said in a sing-song voice, "or someone won't be getting baby time." I patted my belly in emphasis.

"Evil," Rhys muttered but loud enough so I heard him. Suddenly, the two of us burst out laughing. And the rest of the car ride was made in companionable silence.

It took about twenty minutes before we turned off the road. There was a sign, but I didn't catch it as we went up an incline. About a mile in, the road widened and a large log structure with slanted roofs and floor-to-ceiling windows in the middle appeared.

It was perfectly framed by the mountain behind it and the river in front.

"Wow, this is beautiful." I craned my neck to get a better look.

Rhys parked, then turned to me. "Spa day, anyone?"

My eyes widened. "Oh my gosh! Yes, please!" I was huge, and a day of being pampered sounded perfect. I patted my belly again. "Boys, looks like we love Uncle Rhys again."

Rhys snorted and turned the car off. "Boys, your papa is cray-cray. Ignore him."

I laughed and opened the door. Rhys was out of the car and by my side helping me down from the SUV in an instant.

"I so totally would not have thought spa day," I admitted.

"I know," Rhys replied. We started towards the building, and Rhys linked our arms. "But they do a pregnancy massage I thought would be perfect for you."

I moaned. "That sounds wonderful. Between your nephews using my bladder as a trampoline and pushing my organs higher than they should be, a rub-down sounds wonderful."

He hip-checked me. "I thought only Gabe rubbed you down."

"Hardy har har! You're so very funny."

"Thank you," Rhys replied dryly.

He supported me up the stairs, and when we entered the spa, I sighed. It was so welcoming with the light coming in from the back. The layout of the lobby was open, and there was something so welcoming about the space. Light and airy, modern but not cold. Asheville kept surprising and impressing me. This was something I expected in Aspen or Vail, not in a small town in Colorado with under two thousand residents.

I was so proud of my family. I knew how hard Gabe, Austin, Hunter, Graham, and Rhys worked.

A beautiful woman with pale blonde hair and a curvy figure that a Kardashian would kill for came out from behind the counter.

"Rhys." My friend dropped my hand and hugged the woman.

"Brooke, how you doing? As always, you look stunning," Rhys said.

"Such a flatterer." Brooke waved him off.

She looked over to me and smiled. "Kian, we're so glad to have you. I bet you're just dying to get started on that massage and be off your feet."

"Yes, please," I sighed.

"Rhys knows the way to the changing room. Get in your robe, and we'll have you feeling better in no time," Brooke said.

Rhys led me to an elevator and pressed the button. "This place is so nice," I whispered. "I am surprised they have an elevator."

"Mmm, well, it's all about rest and relaxation, and what better way than not to have to climb a flight of stairs?"

"True," I agreed as we stepped in.

When the door closed, I asked, "Who's Brooke?"

"Her family has been here almost as long as ours," Rhys said. "They own about ten acres not too far from here. Her brother is a lawyer in town and close friends with Hunter."

"Is she a bear too?" I asked.

"Yup!" Rhys replied as the elevator door opened. "But her mate is a lion shifter."

"Lion! Woah, I don't know why I never thought of other species."

Rhys chuckled. "I did mention our cousins are wolves, right?"

"I think so." I shook my head. "I'm living a weird, wonderful life."

Rhys snorted and held a door open for me. "Alice, welcome to Wonderland."

"You're such an idiot."

"Who is the idiot, the person that loves the idiot or the idiot themselves?"

I groaned. "I'm ignoring you."

Rhys handed me a robe, and we both went over to the benches and got undressed. Although Rhys had to help me with my pants.

There was a knock on the door, and I slipped my feet into the slippers provided for us as Rhys called, "Come in."

Brooke entered. "Your rooms are ready."

"Are we together?" I asked Rhys.

"Yup. Bestie date, unless you don't want to. I'm sure Brooke can—"

"Nope, I love it," I interrupted him.

We were led into a large room with two massage tables. The rustic vibe was alive in here, but unlike the log color outside, this was lighter reclaimed wood. One of the massage tables had several cushions. The lights were dimmed, and everything looked clean and welcoming.

"Rhys, you know the drill. Disrobe and use the sheet to cover yourself," Brooke said. "Kian, if you don't mind, I'll help you since you can't lay down on your back."

I nodded and slipped my robe off. I'd left my briefs on, so I didn't really mind. Brooke took it and hung it up on the hook on the wall on my side of the room. When she came back, she took my hand and helped me onto the table.

"Lay down on your side," she instructed. "You want your hips right on the edge of the cushion and your arm between the two cushions. We don't want any pressure on your shoulder." She grabbed another cushion and put it between my legs, and I sighed immediately at the relief. It was as good as my pregnancy pillow.

"Comfortable?" she checked.

"Mmm." I sighed, closing my eyes.

"That's exactly what we like to hear."

The next forty-five minutes or so were bliss. My back, shoulders, and even my scalp were rubbed to perfection.

After barely being able to get to sleep, and the fact I couldn't really get comfy, and using the restroom every hour, swollen feet, swollen face, swollen everything kind of struggle, this felt so good.

Getting rubbed on! Seriously, why hadn't I thought

of this? Having my aching feet, lower back, and head massaged was the best ever.

"Rhys, this is the best, most unexpected treat, and I'll love you forever," I sighed.

"Mmm," my best friend moaned. Clearly, he was as blissed-out as I was.

My belly was rubbed with oil but not massaged, which felt nice as well. But Gabe usually did this every night for me.

I must have dozed off because I woke up to Rhys in front of me.

"That good, huh?" He shot me a lopsided grin.

"Perfect," I sighed and met Kian's gaze for a moment. "I feel huge and just uncoordinated, like my body isn't mine. Gabe and I haven't even—" I ducked my head. "What if he doesn't find me attractive anymore?"

Rhys used a finger to lift my chin. "You're joking. Gabe adores you. Like completely besotted with you. I would bet there is not a second that goes by without him thinking about you, Kee. Don't ever doubt that."

"But what about the—you know?"

"I bet it's just because he's being all 'caveman protect my mate' dumb alpha." Rhys snorted.

"You think?" I couldn't help asking.

"I know this." Rhys's voice was firm. "Now, no more worrying, only pampering and then food."

"What would I do without you?" I sighed.

"You'll never have to find out."

RHYS DROPPED me off outside the house and didn't leave until I entered. As if anything could happen to me on the ranch. I waved at him before closing the door.

I checked the kitchen and the living room but didn't find my mate. But I knew he was home since he'd texted earlier, checking on me and asking if he should have dinner waiting. I walked upstairs slowly, and Gabe must have heard me because I saw him coming out of the nursery.

He walked over to me and pulled me into his arms. Gabe kissed me softly. It was slow, sensual, like coming home. Gabe broke the kiss and asked, "How was your day, baby?"

"Great! The spa is beautiful."

"Oh, I'm so glad. I know you've not been sleeping great. I mentioned it to Rhys, and he changed your guys' plan."

"It was just what I needed. What did you get up to in the nursery?"

He took my hand and led me to the room. "Oh, you put the stickers up. It's beautiful." We'd done the nursery in white with one accent wall in olive green. I'd ordered the stickers of teddy bears sitting on clouds and on the moon, dotted with stars of different sizes.

"It's perfect." I turned around and kissed him. "Thank you so much for doing this. I wanted to do it, but my back…"

"That's what I'm here for, my love."

I trailed my hands down his chest. "So I only have to ask?"

Gabe's chest rumbled. "What do you want, baby?"

"You," I said simply, cupping my mate's already hardening dick.

Gabe gripped my neck and tilted my head to the side. He took my lips in a long, hot, tongue-filled kiss that had my body coming to life.

I groaned, sinking into the kiss. And Gabe's hand went under my ass, and he lifted me gently and walked us over to our room. He slowly put me down. Once my feet were on the ground, I tipped my head back to give him access and felt Gabe drop his head and press a kiss to the exposed length of my throat. I moaned softly. With Gabe, I was always transported to a sensual place that I'd never dreamed I'd experience.

A place I'd thought only existed in books.

He kissed me then, driving his tongue into my mouth. I felt my mate's hands on my body, sliding beneath my clothes, baring my flesh to him. He had me naked in no time.

"You're so beautiful, baby," Gabe sighed, nibbling on my neck when I stood in front of him naked. Gabe took his shirt off while I pushed his sweats down. Seeing Gabe naked made me hot and needy. As I took in every inch of his glorious body, every divot and curve, my mouth watered. God, my mate was stunning.

"Get in bed, baby." Gabe helped me in and slid in

behind me, turning to spoon against me, my back to his chest.

"I thought you didn't find me sexy anymore," I admitted in a rushed whisper.

Gabe nipped my shoulder, and a tingle went down my spine. I rolled over to face him, even though it was slow going. When we were face to face, Gabe traced my jaw with his thumb. "I'll always want you, baby. Always." He kissed me softly. "You're my whole world, Kian, and not a second goes by when you're not on my mind, in my heart." He kissed me again, this one deeper. "And trust me, if I could, we would never leave this bed."

My lips curved. "Yeah?"

"Oh yeah!" Gabe nodded.

"Prove it." His eyes darkened, and he growled. I turned on my side again. "Ravish me, mate!"

Gabe kissed the back of my neck with his warm lips as his arms came up around me, pulling me tightly to him. He trailed kisses down along my shoulder, stopping at my claim-mark. My head fell back, and I couldn't stop the moan that escaped. He continued to kiss his way up the side of my neck. I loved the feeling of his beard on my sensitive skin; the feeling sent shocks of pleasure through my body.

He played with my tight nipples, and a groan slipped from between my lips as I lost myself to my mate's touch. Air sawed in and out of my chest as I pushed back and moaned as Gabe's thick cock rubbed over my slick hole.

Gabe's hand traveled down my body, his finger trailing down my hip, my stomach, in a gentle caress. Before dipping between my legs and wrapping his hand around my dick and stroking up and down. I moaned and pushed into his hand.

He nipped my lobe and rolled my nipple between his fingers. "Gabe, please," I begged.

My ass leaked slick as Gabe brought my body to life. He thrust, and his cock teased my hole.

I panted, desperately needing to be filled now.

Gabe must have known how desperate I was because he lifted my leg up and pushed it forward. I tilted my hip and pushed back.

Gabe nipped my shoulder again, and I moaned, and in one thrust, he pushed into my body, filling me completely.

Gabe gave me a second to adjust, until I ground my ass against him. He began to rhythmically rock his hips, making love to me slowly. He held my leg with one hand, keeping it in place while he nuzzled and nipped at my claim-mark while continuing to thrust in and out of my body, hitting my gland on every thrust.

"Please, Gabe," I begged, trying to thrust back, but he held me in place.

My mate knew my body. He knew how to bring me to the edge.

"I'll always want you, Kian. Never doubt that. You're

mine." He never sped up his pace. He fucked me slow and steady until I was a babbling, incoherent mess. "Close. So close," I cried.

His knot thickened, and the pleasure built. It didn't take long until his knot filled my ass and pressed against my gland. My orgasm crashed into me. And I gasped and came, squirting cum all over the sheet in front of me. At the same time, I felt the heat of Gabe's cum filling me up.

Gabe lowered my leg and settled me against him. He wrapped me up in his arms as we waited for his knot to come down.

He nipped my earlobe and whispered, "Never doubt how much I need you, Kian."

22

GABE

"Nothing fits." He gestured to himself. "Look at me. I have my own gravitational field. Can we cancel, pleaseeeeee?" my mate begged.

"My grandparents are here, baby, and they're excited to see you." It wasn't because he didn't want to spend time with my family, but being a week to his due date, I knew it wasn't comfortable for him.

My poor mate. He couldn't even find a comfortable sleeping position anymore. I'd never say it to him.

"I weigh a ton, I can't remember the last time I saw my feet, and I feel like your children are using my insides to play squash." Kian sat on the bench in our walk-in, clothes everywhere. "I have nothing to wear." He looked up at me, and his lips wobbled.

Fuck, not tears. I hated seeing my mate cry. I walked over to my side of the closet and grabbed a T-shirt and some sweats, then walked over to him. I squatted in front of him and pried the pants he held on to out of his hands and tossed them aside.

"We are just going down the road. How about you borrow some of my stuff? You know how much I love you smelling like me." I used the pads of my thumbs to wipe tears from his cheek.

"Baby, it's just the family. They won't care how you look, but if you really don't want to go, we can stay home." Even though I knew Kian would enjoy it, I'd never make my mate do anything that didn't make him happy.

Kian ducked his head. "I'm being a baby, aren't I?"

"Don't say that. Don't even think it. Look at me, baby, please." Kian's head lifted, and our eyes met. "You're pregnant. With twins. In your last month. You don't have to do anything you don't want to. Not for a second."

Kian gave me a lopsided grin. He brushed my beard with his fingers. "I really like when you get all protective."

"Oh, you do, do you?" I teased before pressing a kiss to his lips. As always, my mate responded. "So *Modern Family* and takeout?" I suggested.

"Nope. Family time. I'm in. But I hope no one cares if I look like a bum. Okay mate, help me up."

I grinned, got on my feet, and stretched my hands out for him. Kian placed his hand in mine, and I pulled him up slowly. I hugged my mate to me and kissed the top of his head. "If you want to leave, we'll leave."

Kian nodded against my chest, then pulled back. "You have to help me into my shorts."

"It would be my pleasure." I helped my mate out of the long shirt he had on. It was another one of mine, but with our height difference, it passed for a dress. A little snugger than usual since his belly had popped. I undid a couple of buttons. "Up, babe." He did as I asked, and I lifted it off him. Kian pushed his boxers down, and I helped him out of them.

I couldn't help taking him in—he was gorgeous. I knew he probably didn't feel it, but to me, seeing him ripe with our kids was intoxicating.

He smacked my chest with the back of his hand. "Focus, mate of mine."

"I think I am. On my mate." I smirked at him.

"Later!" he chuckled.

"I'll hold you to it," I assured him, brushing my lips over his.

He pushed me away, laughing. "I need briefs."

"I'm going. I'm going." I walked over to the drawer and grabbed the first pair I could.

We got him dressed and then grabbed his favorite pair of Converse. I helped him sit and then slipped the socks on before his shoes.

When I looked up at him from my position on one knee, he smiled and leaned in for a kiss. "Thanks, babe."

"Anytime, baby." We left the closet, and I made sure to guide him down the stairs since his center of gravity wasn't what it used to be.

"Drive or walk, babe?"

"Ian said walking can get labor going, so walk please," he said.

No problem. I put my hand on his back and held him close as we strolled to my parents' house. It wasn't that long a walk, but we took it slow.

We walked up the stairs, and I stopped outside the door. "Ready?"

Kian frowned and looked up at me. "You're smiling weird! Why are you smiling weird?"

"Hey! There's nothing weird about my smile."

"Just bring him already!" Rhys called out and flung the door open.

"Always so damn impatient," I said to my baby brother.

He shrugged and wiggled his way between Kian and me. "Godfather in the building! Make way."

I laughed and lifted my brother off the ground and put him on my other side, then led my mate into the house.

When we entered the living room, my whole family was there. "Surprise," everyone called out.

Kian gasped, his hands flying to his mouth, and leaned into my side. I wrapped my arm around his waist.

Glancing around, Kian took in the decorations. There was a giant banner that read "Baby Shower."

Streamers of blue, yellow, and green were strewn across the ceiling and hanging down the walls. Small stuffed animals matching the colored streamers were the centerpieces on one of the couches.

The coffee table was covered with stacks of brightly wrapped packages. To the side, there was a double stroller and matching car seats, complete with a giant blue ribbon on top.

"I didn't think…" He sniffed. "We don't really need a shower."

"Of course you do, son." My papa came and stood beside us. "We want to celebrate our grandbabies and you, Kian. And what better way to tell you how much we love you than with gifts and lots of food?"

Kian grinned. "You had me at food."

Everyone laughed, but Grandma came and took Kian, and they headed for the kitchen, thick as thieves. My papa followed them, and my dad approached me.

"You ready, son?" he asked, slinging his arms around my shoulder.

"Yeah, the cribs came last week. They're exactly what I wanted. So the nursery is ready. Kian's baby bag is packed, and we're ready to go."

Hunter stepped up to us. "Yeah, I love it; the baby cubs playing around a human sitting cross-legged and a family of older bears watching out for them."

My grandpa walked up and handed me a glass. "Good job, son."

But then he shared a look with my papa that had me asking, "What? What?" and looking between them.

Papa slapped my back. "Trust me, even when you think you are, you're never ready."

"And two in one go," Grandpa chimed in. "Urs give you strength."

I laughed. "I'm not worried. Between Grandma and Papa, I have a feeling Kian and I won't get any baby time."

"Don't forget Rhys," Hunter added.

"Or you." I raised a brow at my brother.

He shrugged but didn't deny it.

The door opened, and Graham walked in with a cake box in his hand. "Am I late? Did I miss it?" my brother asked.

"Nope, right on time," I reassured him.

"I can't believe we managed to keep this a secret all these weeks!" I heard Rhys say. He came back with my mate, who now had a cute little bowl with popcorn and M&Ms.

"I don't know what to say." Kian swiped at a tear trickling down his cheek. "Thank you all so much."

"Oh honey," Grandma said from behind him. "You never have to thank us, baby."

"I do," Kian sniffed. "I didn't think I would ever find another family after losing my papa. Then Rhys…" His voice caught, and our eyes met. "And then Gabe." I walked over to him, and he stepped into my arms. My mate took a moment before lifting his head. "All of you. I don't know how I deserved you." He shook his head and laughed, swiping at tears in his eyes. "But I don't care. You're all mine, and I'm never giving you up." Kian's smile was watery. "You're mine. You're stuck with me."

I saw my dad and my grandpa swipe at their eyes.

Finally, the silence was broken when Graham said, "And I'm the favorite 'cause I brought cake."

Kian beamed at my brother. "Definitely."

For the next hour or so, Kian made sure to speak with each of my brothers, my papa, dad, grandpa, and grandma. I loved the happy look in his eyes. And I knew my family could never replace the one he lost. My heart broke every time I saw him standing by the urn that now took pride of place in our living room, telling them about his life. All I could do was thank them for giving me Kian. And hope that they thought I was good enough for him.

There was clapping, and I looked over and saw Rhys standing in front of the TV. He didn't stop till he had everyone's attention.

"Now that everyone has chatted and stuffed their faces, it's time to get to the opening of the presents."

"You guys have already bought so much." Kian looked around the room.

"There's no such thing," Grandma said as she got on her feet and grabbed the first gift she could get her hands on and placed it in Kian's lap.

For the next hour or so, Kian opened presents. Even my brothers, and Papa and Grandpa oohed and aahed at everything he held up.

We got a lot of boxes of diapers and baskets filled with baby bath wash, shampoo, and lotions. A lot of bodysuits because apparently, we couldn't have enough.

The smile on Kian's face got bigger and bigger, and I loved seeing it.

A lot of the clothes were given in pairs. To be honest, there were a lot of matching outfits. Our kids would probably never have to repeat clothes. Although I would bet, just like he had already with all the other gifts we'd received, some would find their way to the omega house.

Like I needed more reasons to fall for Kian.

Once Kian yawned for the fifth time, everyone told me to get him home. They promised to deliver all the presents.

When I tucked Kian in bed, he whispered, "I really wish my papa and daddy got a chance to meet all of you." He yawned. "They would have loved you so much."

I sighed and kissed him on his forehead. "I love you so much, Kian."

"BABE." I was being shaken awake. "I need the bathroom."

I'd been so attuned to Kian, I was up in a moment

and on his side of the bed, helping him up. He took a step. "Oh no, I peed myself," he cried.

"It's okay, baby," I soothed him. "It's okay."

I frowned when I realized the back of the pajama pants he wore was soaked too.

"I think your water broke, baby."

"What!" Kian gasped. "But I didn't feel it."

"I think the soaked pants are kind of a dead give-away," I pointed out.

"We still have over a week," Kian reminded me.

"Well, I guess the babies aren't very good with the whole time thing yet."

I lowered him back to the bed. "I'll go get you a change of clothes, baby," I said.

Kian nodded absently, his hand rubbing his belly in a circular motion.

I hurried to the walk-in and grabbed sweats and a T-shirt and put them on. I also grabbed another pair of pajama pants and a T-shirt from my closet for Kian.

"Shoes." I grabbed slides and dropped them on the ground, shoving my feet in, and a pair for Kian too.

I'd read during labor, loose-fitted, comfortable items were best.

"Shit." The first thing I was supposed to do was call Ian. I hurried back to the room, and Kian looked up at me. I kissed his cheek before telling him to lift his arms. Like a puppet, he did as I asked. I pulled his shirt over his head and helped him wiggle out of his soiled pants.

"We're having a baby," Kian whispered.

"I know, love, and everything will be just fine, babe." I kept my voice gentle and calm. "This is the moment we've been waiting for, huh?"

Recognition registered once he processed my words, and he started nodding.

"We're having a baby." Kian's voice was awe-filled.

"Yes, my love." I got him into the clean, dry clothes and then helped Kian stand.

A determined look replaced the dazed one. "Let's go meet our babies."

I grabbed my phone and keys to the SUV. I stopped in the nursery for the bags, and we were on our way.

THE CONTRACTION SUBSIDED. Kian opened his eyes and gazed at me.

"Breathe, baby," I instructed, pushing his hair back. Kian expelled a deep, cleansing breath.

The birthing suite didn't really look like a hospital room. The walls were a mint green color. There was a plush couch sat opposite the bed under the large window and a small coffee table.

The room was large enough to hold his whole family and then some, but it was just us. Kian and I wanted to share this moment together.

Of course, the room also had all the necessary medical stuff, but the atmosphere was definitely geared towards more of a homey, comfortable, and incredibly relaxing vibe.

Our Omega Obstetrics department at the hospital was fantastic. We took great pride in catering to our omegas.

As my mate went through contractions, all I could do was stand beside him, holding his hand and mopping his brow.

"How're you doing, hon?" Patrick, our nurse, who'd been at our side since we arrived, asked as he studied the fetal monitor beside the bed.

"I'm good," Kian managed between panting breaths.

"And how's the pain?" he asked.

"Uhm, manageable." He managed a small smile.

I placed a kiss on his brow. Wishing I could bear the pain for him. "You're amazing, baby," I whispered. "I am so in awe of you."

Kian kissed me and whispered against my lips, "I love you, Gabe, so much."

"If you want the epidural, Kian, we're about to reach the point of no return," Patrick said. "Unlike shifters, you won't burn it off as fast. It could help."

"I'm good," my mate said. "At least I think so." He laughed. "Let's hope I don't regret it soon."

The next hour or so was spent wiping sweat from Kian's brow and holding his hand. The contractions continued to progress, growing more intense.

Finally, Ian came into the room, but my mate was preoccupied with a particularly strong contraction.

And he groaned and squeezed my hand so much I actually winced.

"I see things are progressing," Ian called out as he walked into the room. He walked up to the bed and glanced at the monitor before focusing on Kian. "How're you doing?"

"Apart from the whole insides being twisted?" Kian smiled was pained. "They're definitely getting stronger."

"Looks like your little ones are anxious to meet you two, like their dad, always ahead of everyone else," Ian teased, but before I could reply, another contraction crept up on Kian.

Kian moaned and squirmed on the bed as the contraction hit.

Ian checked the fetal monitor. "Everything looks good," he said as he sat on the side of the bed. "And how are our dads holding up?"

I met my friend's gaze. "Waiting for my family to be safe. Hoping my mate isn't in pain for long."

"I know." Ian smiled. "Good job, alpha, keeping your bear in check. I know what it's like watching your mate go through this. Feeling helpless…" He shook his head.

"Took the words out my mouth," I muttered.

I had a whole new appreciation and respect for my mate and every omega. I kissed Kian's forehead.

He gave me a weak smile.

Ian pushed the cover covering my mate's lower half.

He winked at me. "Try to keep your bear in check; I need to check your mate's dilation status."

"Don't worry, doc. I'll smack him if he misbehaves," Kian got out before taking several deep breaths. I focused on Kian's face, not looking at what was going on down there. My bear was barely holding on.

"You're almost there, Kian," Ian announced. "Now, we just gotta wait for one of your little guys to find their way into the birth canal, and soon, you'll be holding your babies."

The intensity of the contractions didn't let up. I had a feeling we were just getting started.

A contraction racked my mate's body, and he screamed. My bear roared, wanting to protect our mate but not knowing how.

Less than forty-five minutes later, it was time, and Kian was very vocal.

"It hurts," Kian cried as his legs were lifted into the stirrups on either side of the bed, ready for delivery.

"That means your little guys are about ready to get this show on the road," Ian said.

Kian moaned and whimpered, thrashing his head from side to side. "Oh! Oh! Oh!" he repeated over and over, squeezing my hand for dear life.

"I need you to push for me, Kian," Ian said softly.

"I'm not ready." Kian shook his head. "Not ready. Hurts bad. So bad."

"Ian," I growled. "What about the epidural?"

My friend shook his head. "Too late to give him

anything. But his body knows exactly what to do. And once they're out, no more pain."

I clenched my fist at my side. Fuck! I hated not being able to fix this for my mate.

"Kian," Ian said, "the faster you get to pushing, the faster you can hold your babies."

"You missed the part in between, doc." Kian tried to joke, but it was followed by a groan so deep I felt it in my heart.

"Baby," I whispered against his head, my hand rubbing his belly. "You can do this. You're so strong, Kian. So damn strong."

Kian cried out as another contraction hit.

"Okay, Kian, on the count of three, you're going to give me a push. Okay?" Ian instructed.

Kian nodded and shook his head at the same time. "One...two...three, deep breath, Kian, and give me a push," Ian demanded.

Kian drew in a deep breath and bore down.

"That's it," Ian praised.

My mate cried, "Ohhhhh." Until his back hit the pillow again.

Less than a minute later, Ian said, "All right, Kian, here comes another contraction." I picked up the cloth from the bed and wiped his brow.

"Hee, hee, hee...hoo, hoo, hoo." My mate breathed.

"Good job with the breathing," Ian said. "Deep breath and push, Kian."

I watched my mate do as instructed.

"Push, Kian," Ian said. And my mate did until he could rest again.

"I take back the whole big family thing." Kian's smile was strained. "Two. Two is good."

I laughed and nodded. "Whatever you want, baby."

"Deep breath and push," Ian commanded. "That's it. We have a head crowning."

Kian bore down, and a scream was ripped from him. After a deep breath, he growled impressively. "Get 'em out. Out!" Kian shouted.

"I need another push, Kian. You're doing so good," Ian praised. "Give me another big one, and the head should be out. Big push, Kian."

Kian whimpered and panted.

"Here comes the contraction, Kian," Ian said. "Big push, let's get this little one out."

"Ooooooooooooooooh," Kian cried without pausing as he bore down.

"Rest, Kian, the head is out," he said. "Deep breath so we can get the rest of him here."

My mate did as he was told, and I talked nonsensically to him. There was a plop, and Kian's head fell back. "Congratulations, it's a boy."

A bloody, gooey blob was plunked on Kian's belly, and instinctively, my mate reached for our baby.

Patrick used something in his mouth and up his nostrils, and I watched his every move. This was my mate and our son. My family. "It's to suck out the mucus," the nurse said like he knew how I was feeling.

The next thing I knew, a cry filled the room from the beautiful gooey blob on my mate.

"Hey, baby," Kian sobbed, holding him against his body. The goo was wiped off my son, and I lowered my head to them.

I kissed Kian and whispered, "Thank you." I stroked a finger down my son's back. "Hey, baby boy. Is he okay?" I asked Ian.

Gods, my throat was tight.

"Ten fingers, ten toes," Ian confirmed. "Would you like to cut the cord?"

I met my mate's eyes, and he smiled and nodded.

I moved so I could grip the scissors Ian also held and cut through my son's cord.

"You're doing so well," Ian praised Kian. "Patrick will have to take him to get cleaned up for you."

Kian's forehead creased, and I felt his worry. I looked at the nurse.

"We just need a few minutes; he won't leave the room," Patrick said. "We'll get him weighed and measured. Give him a quick checkup, and he'll be right back."

I met my mate's eye and nodded, and then he finally released his hold on our son.

I kissed him and reminded him how much I loved him.

Ian kept his eyes on the monitor.

"Is he okay?" Kian's eyes went to it too, even

though, like me, he probably didn't know what it meant.

"Everything is good," Ian replied. And even I found myself breathing out. "He'll let us know when he's ready to join his brother."

Patrick returned with our little guy bundled up. "I've got a little boy ready to meet his daddy." He came over to my side. "Here you go, Daddy," he said before handing a bundle wrapped tight in a blanket with race cars and a white hat peeking out the top to me.

My body locked up tight for a moment until I remembered I knew what to do.

I cradled my son in the crook of my arm, and tears welled in my eyes. "Hello, son," I whispered, rocking back and forth and speaking softly to our son.

I placed a gentle kiss on the top of our baby's head and didn't even try to wipe away a tear that trickled down my cheeks.

"He's so beautiful, perfect," I sighed. I never wanted to let him go.

When I looked over at my mate, I saw tears streaming down his cheeks.

"Beau," Kian whispered. It was one of the names we'd picked.

"Are you Beau?" I cooed at my son. He sucked his lips, and I sighed. "I think that's a yes."

I sat on the edge of the bed and propped our son up so Kian could get a good look at him.

"Say 'hi' to your papa, son," I said, meeting his gaze.

"He's the most amazing person in the whole world." Leaning over, I placed a sweet kiss on his lips.

Kian brushed the back of his finger along our son's cheek.

"Looks like your brother is taking his sweet time," I said to our little one.

Ian laughed. "He'll come when he's ready, but I bet it'll be any time now."

Less than twenty minutes later, the contractions came back strong. Our other son came quicker and smoother than his older brother.

Rhett and Beau. Our babies were here, and they were perfect, and I would protect them and Kian with my last breath.

23

KIAN

I fastened Beau into his car seat while Gabe got Rhett ready. I smiled as my mate tucked the blanket around him. I would never get tired of the look of awe he had when he held our babies. Like he couldn't believe they were real. Then he would get this fierce look on his face, and I knew our boys would always be safe.

The love in Gabe's face was so palpable that it made me fall for him all over again.

This family I had was everything and more than I'd dreamed of when I'd packed my bags and left Philadelphia.

Gabe and now our babies and the whole Hallbjørn clan. I liked to think Papa and Daddy had been looking out for me. They'd sent me to the family I needed since they couldn't be here. Without Papa's words telling me never to settle, I might have never found him. Never had our little ones. Which, even after five or so hours of labor, I'd never trade for the world.

Although next time I would definitely be taking the drugs.

My heart was full and overflowing as I counted my blessings all through the ride home.

It was the little things, too, like my mate glancing in the mirror, checking we were okay as he drove.

"We're good, babe," I reassured him from my position in the backseat between the two car seats.

"I know." Gabe met my eyes in the mirror for a second. "Still, precious cargo on board and all."

Like that.

I smiled before adjusting the hat on Beau's head. The ride home, which took fifteen minutes usually, took us about twenty-five. I didn't have the heart to tease my mate. Because I knew how he felt, holding our little guys in my arms, seeing how small and fragile they were. I wanted to protect them from everything. If driving slower helped my mate feel like he was protecting us, then who was I to complain?

When we pulled into the ranch, I put my hand on each of my sons' tummies. "Welcome home, little ones," I whispered. "You have an amazing family who can't wait to meet you, love you."

"I bet my family is already at the house, waiting." Gabe and I shared a knowing smile.

"I don't mind." Beau opened his eyes and stretched out his hands like a cat stretching. I put my finger in his hand, and his tiny little grip was surprisingly strong. I said a prayer that nothing would happen to Gabe or me, that he would never know that pain. I shook off that feeling, burying it for later. I couldn't let fear creep into this day. "I can't wait for everyone to meet them."

"I have a feeling you won't get to hold them much once the family lays eyes on them." Gabe laughed.

I loved that there were so many people, that they'd never feel alone. Truth was, from the moment we'd had that ultrasound that said we would have twins, I'd been so happy because they'd always have each other. And if my new family was any indication, they'd always stick close and have a home to come home to.

The moment Gabe parked in front of our home, he took his seat belt off and turned to face me.

He took my hand in his. "You okay, baby?" I didn't miss the concern and love written all over his face.

I nodded and looked between our sons. "I'm just so happy," I admitted.

A huge grin spread across his face. "So am I, baby. So am I."

Before we could say any more, the door to my left was pulled open, and Rhys was standing there.

"You guys have forever to make googly eyes at each other. I want to meet my nephews and godsons."

"May I?" Rhys stroked down Rhett's cheek.

I nodded, and like a pro, he unstrapped my son and

lifted him, supporting his head before bringing him to his chest.

He lifted the baby so he could rub his cheek over Rhett's head, and I saw my friend breathe in his nephew like he was learning his scent. His eyes teared up as he rocked him. "He's so beautiful, Kee."

I grinned at him. "We think so too."

The other door opened, and it was Jon. "I have a feeling Rhys won't let me at my grandson, but lucky for me, I've got two."

"Beau would love to meet his Pop-pop." Instead of lifting Beau out, Jon released the car seat from its base and lifted it out. "Easier for you to get out, hun. I know how you must be feeling." We shared a commiserating look.

I loved our little guys, but I felt like I'd been through the wringer.

Our kids were taken inside without us. Then it was just Gabe and me. "How're you feeling, baby?" he asked.

"Exhausted, but so very happy." I sat with my legs dangling from the car, and I rested my head against my mate's chest.

"We're parents," I sighed. "Can you believe it?"

"Some days, I still can't believe you're here." Gabe joined our foreheads. "And I thank the Gods for that, but then I held our sons, and I was terrified because I'm so damn happy. There's no misery to balance the happiness. I just want to hold the three of you close and never let go." I wiped the tears that trailed down my mate's cheeks.

"We're going to have an amazing life. Our kids will too," I said firmly and said a prayer to God that he listened and called on my parents to watch out for their grandbabies, my mate, and me. "What part of 'you're stuck with me' don't you get, alpha?"

The corner of his mouth quirked up.

"We're gonna have dirty diapers, sleepless nights from teething, first steps. First word, which of course will be Papa." That got a full smile. "We're going to be there for all their firsts, and then one day, we'll be the ones grabbing our grandbabies out of the car, playing keep away."

"Promise," my mate whispered in a choked voice.

"I promise." I wanted every moment with this man, and I would work every day to make it so. Because there was no doubt in my mind that my stubborn alpha would show up for me every single day, and I planned to enjoy a whole lot of them with him.

We finally went into the house, and my whole family was there. Of course, they'd gone all out. There was enough food for the next few days. The co-sleeper had been moved to our room. I sat in my mate's arms and watched as my sons were fawned over and thanked my lucky stars, I'd found my way home.

EPILOGUE - GABE

"I'M SURPRISED BY HOW WELL THE DIRECT ORDERS ARE doing. I shouldn't be because my mate and Rhys did such a wonderful job," I mused, looking over the numbers for the last quarter. We'd rolled out Kian and Rhys's joint effort just eight months ago, and it had definitely shown in our profits. "Who knew people preferred to grab their Thanksgiving turkeys and Christmas hams online and not have to go to the store? And the bundles are doing so well."

"Rhys and Kian," Bailey replied. "And they knew people wouldn't stop there. We've not had a single order since we started. It's like most people get on, and they figure if I'm buying this, I may as well buy in bulk."

I laughed. "I guess I underestimated the convenience factor."

"Yup, we should just let the omegas run things. They seem to know better," Bailey pointed out.

"I will be telling my mate you said that," I told my assistant.

She snorted. "It's the truth."

"Yeah," I agreed. "Because I never thought our company would ever do faux meat, but of course, the profit margin on it has definitely been worthwhile."

"Getting a couple of shifter influencers didn't hurt," she added. "And I thought Kian told you not to call it faux-meat anymore. They're meat substitutes."

"I know. I know." I waved her off. "Our non-meat-eating shifters have been very happy."

"Like I said, the omegas are smarter than you," Bailey said.

"This is exactly what Rhys wanted when he started this whole rebrand scheme." I couldn't help smiling thinking about that day almost two years ago. I would never stop being grateful Rhys had out-stubborned me because my mate and family were everything to me.

Kian was not only an amazing mate; he was also a wonderful father. And between him and Rhys, our business had grown.

"The website traffic was over fifty-thousand, and I think we can triple that for Easter," Bailey added, studying the numbers on her tablet. "But if we want to deliver direct-to-door past our backyard, we may have to revisit opening CBF warehouses in certain locations."

"I'll discuss it with the family in the next meeting, see what they think. I wouldn't want us expanding too fast and running into problems. The western United States is already a lot of ground."

We talked a little more about the business, going over what was needed and making sure everything was running smoothly.

With this being my last minute today, I left just before six. Sometimes, I thought about my old self still here till nine, no one to go home to. And even though my house was a lot louder, definitely stickier, I wouldn't change it or trade it for anything else.

I didn't dread going home to the oppressive quiet. Nope, there were usually people screaming *Daddy* as soon as I walked in the door and Kian looking at me like no one ever had. I would never tire of seeing the happiness in his eyes when I walked in the door.

I pulled into the garage and jumped out of my UTV. When I entered the kitchen, there was no one there, and then I heard the voices coming from the backyard through the open sliding door in the kitchen.

I left my laptop bag on the counter and followed the sounds; I walked out and saw my mate sitting cross-legged on a carpet, two little bear cubs against his thigh.

"They shifted," I gasped in awe.

Kian smiled up at me. "Yeah. I was trying to keep them shifted until you came home."

I lowered my head and kissed my mate softly. "Hey, baby," I whispered.

Kian's eyes crinkled. "Hey, babe."

Our boys woke up and saw me and immediately shuffled over, nipping at my ankles. I grinned and squatted so they could reach me, and I pulled both my boys into my arms.

"You're so smart," I cooed at them. At eighteen months, they were early on their first shift.

Beau managed to balance on his hind legs but not for long, and Kian praised him. Rhett rolled on his back, and I rubbed his belly. Gods, could my life be any better?

Kian gave me a knowing smile. "You're dying to change and play with them, aren't you?"

I grinned. "You know me so well, mate."

Kian held our little guys as I got undressed quickly. I walked down the patio steps and let the shift overtake me, and Kian walked down with a bear cub in each arm. He stopped in front of me, and I leaned my head against his belly.

Kian put our sons down and pushed his hand through my fur. I purred, and my mate laughed and stepped back. "Go have fun with our sons."

I ran and was chased by two little cubs. Yeah, I thanked Urs that Rhys had been his usual self because I wouldn't have any of this.

∾

Read Austin's story next. His Patient Bear, the second book in the Bears Of Asheville series, is available to Pre-Order Now.

ALSO BY SKYE R. RICHMOND

Billionaire Alphas Series

Unsuitable Omega

Undercover Omega

Temporary Omega

Unforgettable Omega

Unexpected Alpha

Rescued Alpha

Billionaire Alphas Books 1 - 4

Billionaire Alphas Book 1 - 4 Epilogues

Whitfell Brothers

Malek

Malachi

Mikhail

Marcellus

Wildwood Mates

Safe In His Arms

Home In His Arms

Whole In His Arms

The Lost Wolves (With Skyler Snow)

Betrayed

Hunted

Healing

Wild

Vale Valley Season Five (Multi-Author Series)

Omega On His Doorstep

Bears Of Asheville

His Patient Bear

WRITING AS RHELAND RICHMOND

Stories Of Us

A Family For Keeps

His Instant Family

Christmas For Keeps - A Stories Of Us Christmas

The Family We Make: A Valentine's Novella

A Family Of His Own

Amber Falls

Stranded With His Boss

Forever With His Boss

Holding On To His Manny

Naughty Or Nice

Dear Daddy, Please Trust Me

Strictly Off Limits (With Skyler Snow)

Forbidden

Fragile

ABOUT THE AUTHOR

For as long as she can remember Skye had her nose stuck in a book, getting lost in the world of someone else's creation (She still does). Her love for writing came from her love for reading. She could never have one without the other.

Writing was always a hobby and a cathartic experience for her. There are many stories lost to the never to be completed or published pile but needed to be written at the time.

Just a girl that loved stories so much she decided to write hers.

She would love to hear from her readers and learn more about Y'all. So if you get a chance... Get in touch.

www.rhelandrichmond.com/contact

Would you like to get updates about future releases from Skye R. Richmond?

Sign up for my newsletter.

Connect with Rheland on social media:

facebook.com/SkyeRRichmond
twitter.com/RhelandRichmond
instagram.com/rhelandrichmond
amazon.com/author/skyerichmond
bookbub.com/authors/skye-r-richmond